PRAISE FOR

Too Much Dark Matter, Too Little Gray

"…a deep, thoughtful work emphasizing philosophy and high concept. Each of its stories has something distinct to say."

—*The Review Hart*

"*Too Much Dark Matter, Too Little Gray* is chock full of gooey mind-bending goodness. Mike Robinson delivers equal parts of scares and the bizarre with wit and style. Put him on your list of authors to watch."

—Guy Anthony De Marco, Bram Stoker Award® Finalist

"Deliciously off-kilter…The short stories in this book bear a strong resemblance to the "New Wave" science fiction of the 1960s. …[and] display a fine literary craftsmanship flavored with subtlety, irony, color, depth, passion, distinctive style and real original feeling. …Inventive, stylish and polished, they entertain and stimulate."

—Aaron C. Brown, Top 1000 Amazon Reviewer

too much DARK MATTER too little GRAY

A COLLECTION OF WEIRD FICTION

MIKE ROBINSON

AUDACIOUS PUBLISHING, LLC

Los Angeles, CA

TOO MUCH DARK MATTER, TOO LITTLE GRAY:
A Collection of Weird Fiction `

3rd Edition Copyright © 2025 by Mike Robinson
(Original 1st Edition © 2014 by Mike Robinson)
(2nd Edition © 2021 by Mike Robinson)

ISBN: 978-1-7372712-2-2

Cover Design: Damonza.com
Interior Design: Polgarus Studio

Audacious Publishing, LLC
Los Angeles, CA

ALSO BY MIKE ROBINSON

The Prince of Earth
Skunk Ape Semester
Dreamshores: Monster Island
The Atheist
Dishonor Thy Father (with M.J. Richards)
Hurakan's Chalice (with Aiden James)
Walking the Dusk
Ancient Tides Ashore

ENIGMA OF TWILIGHT FALLS TRILOGY
The Green-Eyed Monster
Negative Space
Waking Gods

Select titles also available on Audible and Audio CD

"They are ill-discoverers, those that think there is no land when they can see nothing but sea."

— Francis Bacon

Contents

Hero's Journey

Extended its full length, the dining table now accommodated a supercluster of porcelain galaxies. Salty golden nebulae of chips. Constellations of candy. Huge rugged clusters of fried chicken. In sparse assortment were fruits and vegetables, and toward the wall ruled the kingdom of the sweets. Or, to continue the astronomy metaphors, what I called the diabetic black hole.

"No touching, Pat, and no eating," demanded my roommate. "Not till people come."

It was New Year's Eve 2000, on the real verge of the millennium. My roommate at the time was an older, rotund Russian named Mikhailov. With his looks and his jolly manner, he could have passed for a younger, more carefree Kris Kringle. Somewhat pathetically, he had a strong desire to "party American," and so loved throwing shindigs, though he relied on my friends to fill them. Maybe one or two coworkers of his came. I never remembered their names.

I'm not necessarily complaining. As an astrophysics doctoral candidate, my eyes were far better acquainted with numbers than faces. It was good that he pushed me to be more social, especially when my friends were slyly jumping ship. I didn't even notice what was happening, but of course

1

I realize now the problem was me. I was young and totally absorbed with my work. If anyone couldn't match my "bigger, grander" ways of thinking, they were unworthy of my time and notice. I felt I'd conquered the world around me—I knew its tricks, knew the secrets under the hood, and the next cave of wonders could only be the heavens—and so I rattled on about philosophy and cosmology, the Big Issues.

Unlike many of my friends, I had little interest in the ceaseless babble of earthly affairs: politics, celebrities, sports, fashion, all those squeaks in this great cosmic symphony. My friends never actually said much to me, but eventually it only took one remark and an accompanying look from a blind date to awaken me to that same look in my friends' faces, the look that said, "Is this *all* you're ever going to talk about?"

That night, I resolved to have fun—the last thousand years were ending, after all. Plus my mouth was watering for beer. Much of what Mikhailov had out in the way of drinks didn't appeal to me: a glistening forest of vodka bottles, some bourbon, rum, and two bottles of white wine. I offered to head to the store to load up further and, with big-toothed appreciation, he clapped my back and gestured zealously at the door, ushering me on my little quest. When his back was turned, I snagged a chocolate chip cookie for the road.

The store was only a block away, and normally I would have taken my car to go such a short distance. But today felt different. Only a half hour of daylight remained in the century—in the millennium! It was an exceptional winter day in Los Angeles, and I'd experienced it all behind a window. I resolved to walk, stretch a bit, and get some fresh smog. I thought about grabbing my cell phone from my room, but figured I wouldn't need it for such a short jaunt.

The sky was a luminous blue, a band of twilight between the redness at the horizon and the coming night. The air had that ripe, wintry smell.

As I walked, my brain became a black hole, sucking into oblivion all else around me as it reran current issues I was having in my work, which dealt, fittingly, with black holes. I'd been obsessed with the phenomenon since I was a kid and realized they were *real*, not cool ingredients in science fiction. To me nothing in the universe was as mysterious. To think that these invisible gluttons of light truly hang out there as open wounds in nature, bullying physical logic, possibly existing as passages to some other realm or realms into which they excrete their voluminous intake—it jazzed me. Hell, these things eat *stars*. If that isn't a monster to end all those of the comic panel or movie screen, I don't know what is.

The din of my thoughts receded once I reached the store. There was more pressing business afoot.

I started trolling the aisles, picking out the booze. Something was amiss, but I found it hard to focus past the huge selection of bottles and six-packs before me. Everything looked good.

Having grabbed a basket, I realized I'd need more space, so I retrieved a cart and wheeled away, loading up.

The sky darkened as I approached the counter.

I paid, bagged everything, trying to ignore a strange buzzing deep within my very marrow, as if my body were gearing up, being primed for something.

Wheeling the cart out into the funereal lighting of the streetlamps, I stopped.

You walked here, dolt. Remember?

A little panicky flare went up in me, but I reasoned that I could just take the shopping cart. It wasn't exactly legal, or ethical, but I'd seen plenty of homeless people with them, and my parents' neighbor used to bring them home all the time.

Except when I got to the edge of the parking lot, the wheels locked up and I could go no farther. I saw the sign at the front of the cart which had been there the entire time, unnoticed: *Equipped with Anti-Theft Distance Locks.* I lowered my head. Shook it.

And my cell phone sat comfortably on my desk.

Of course, it's easy now to say I should've just asked the clerk to watch the stuff for me as I went back to get my car. At the time I wasn't sure I could do that, and, furthermore, my defensive claws were always up, protecting my ego and my intellect, even from myself. My entire life I've had a phobia of being perceived as stupid, and have gone to great lengths to market myself as anything but. This includes studying astrophysics and addressing Big Issues whenever I could, because just attempting such things tends to impress. Even with confidence that someone was "below" me intellectually, as the hazy-eyed clerk clearly was, I couldn't present to him such a memorable slip-up when he didn't know me. To counteract it, I would probably have to wax in-depth on cosmic inflation.

So I went back in and bought a big plastic container and

transferred everything into it. I thought this would prove a decent solution, and I could get a little workout carrying it back. But the weight of the liquor-filled container was positively Titan in scope, enviable only to Atlas.

Terribly out of shape, I managed to make it only to the sidewalk before my arms shuddered their complaints and I set it down.

Meanwhile, something was happening, and I couldn't tell if it was happening to me, or everyone else, or both. The feeling was tangible enough to be undeniable, intangible enough to be indescribable. Something heightened in the interface between me and the surrounding buildings, the trees, these passing cars and people: the very electricity of their existence, and their connection to me, shot up in wattage. All things assumed a strange veneer. The alleyway was a cement River Styx, cut long through the blinking firelights of Hades.

And I had to haul this damn container.

Put yourself out, I thought. Divorce mind from matter. It's not that heavy. You're young. Charge ahead and do it.

First, I had to cross the street. Deciding to play it safe, I shoved the container on down to the crosswalk. The scraping-crunching cacophony of the plastic against pavement made it seem as though I were ripping through space-time itself. Indeed, with these queer sensations, such a thing appeared rather possible.

Already I was hot, my breathing labored. Muscles unused since childhood were wrenched awake, painfully so. Mild dizziness set in and stars peppered my vision, shooting around like little meteors. I closed my eyes, waiting for them to stop, but they seemed to enjoy the black canvas of my eyelids even more, and swiftly gathered about like sentient pebbles to form silvery pupils, wide and peering back at me. They blinked. I snapped mine open.

The signal flashed *Walk*. With a deep breath I picked up the container, in mortal combat with gravity, and heaved it fast as I could across the intersection. From dark windshields the faces in the cars followed me, and in one I caught something wet, a shimmering, amphibious complexion and hollow orange eyes—foreign and unknown, but surely a trick of light as a quick second glance confirmed nothing of the first.

I reached the other side and rested, breath pulsing, heart a thunderous din, banging and clamoring to be let out, to join another body perhaps, another brain, one not so dimwitted or addled.

My left arm ached, so for a short while I dragged the container with my right. Stopping to rest again by a shadowed alcove, I noticed a homeless man sitting against the stucco wall. He too was staring at me, and I stared at him behind my wavering, watery vision.

"Happy Millennium," he said to me.

I didn't respond, too mesmerized by the unfolding sight: he was being broken down into smaller and smaller constituents, pore by pore, molecule by molecule, cell by cell. Each piece glowed faintly, and was strung together by threads of light that were, most astonishingly, maintained by thousands of tiny nymph-like creatures hovering around him, ensuring his cohesion. Much as with a crowd of people, I gleaned thousands of different personalities in these entities—some were anxious, others jokey, others lazy and all things between and beyond.

I pulled away and shoved the container onward, scraping it to the mouth of the alleyway where once again I had to stop to catch my breath.

What the hell is happening to me?

My mind scrambled for answers. In the flurry of possibilities—which included tumors, schizophrenia, or degenerative eye disease—I remembered the chocolate chip cookie I'd had going out. I recalled Mikhailov remarking to me, while I was characteristically distracted with my studies and preparing breakfast, that he was going to secure a dozen mushroom cookies from a friend, all for New Year's. "A wild time," he'd said. "Crazy, crazy." He must have set them out, and I must have taken one. I centered on this explanation, recognizing it as the most probable and also the most assuaging, even though I'd never before taken a psychedelic.

Yet even this self-assured answer did little to reduce a paralyzing loneliness that cut through me, a stony sense of isolation, of being stranded, despite being some hundred and fifty yards from home. I wouldn't get there, I thought. And if I didn't destroy myself, then something else would.

But nothing's here.

Right?

The alleyway was desolate, quiet, lit only by the occasional window of adjacent apartments and the icy Cyclopean glare of the moon. I kept my head down as I shoved the container forward, heaving long step by long step, yard by yard, all to the clanging, jingling score of the bottles within knocking about one another.

I noticed other things, though I tried not to. Perched upon the corner of one of the apartment buildings, peering down on me with faint ember eyes, was a large, winged creature, its outline resembling that of a gargoyle even as it was more feathery in makeup, like a giant owl. In its stare I peered through a tunnel billions of light-years long, perhaps to the flickering embryo of the Big Bang.

Then it spread its wings, briefly eclipsing the moon until its whole image blipped like a television with bad reception and, with nary a sound, it sank seamless into the dark behind it.

Keep moving—keep moving—

Pushing the container proved the fastest mode of travel, though I was sure it was tearing up the bottom. I stopped at intervals to ease my muscles and catch my breath, struggling not to make much eye contact with things I only began to sense were around me. Yet even from the blankness of the ground I couldn't escape the strangeness, as the pavement started bubbling beneath my feet, popping, roiling like black lava. I was terrified I might be standing on a sinkhole, or some undiscovered fault line ready to pry open the rugged maw of the planet.

I pressed on, trying not to sob, telling myself none of this was real, though such a mantra became a useless, stale prayer as I struggled toward my destination. Even if these things weren't physically real, even if they were drug-induced, that still meant my brain was making them, that they existed as creations engineered by some haywire Dr. Frankenstein working deep in my psyche.

At last I made to the other end of the alley, watched by things felt but unseen. A towel hanging over a balcony became, momentarily, a waterfall. A tree assumed the likeness of some thirty-foot rodent, perfectly still and smiling at me. I thought, No, that's ridiculous! That's not a rodent. The tree is having fun with me. It's doing impressions.

Thankfully, since I lived on the ground floor, getting to my place required no stairs. Rest was only a gate and a short corridor's walk away. This gave me the final surge of determination needed, once the gate was open, to pick up the damn container and carry it the rest of the way—one last masochistic burn before I could partake of its contents and clobber Mikhailov for the cookie.

The hallways of my complex were bone white. The walls were splashed with shadows, bobbing heads and arms gelled into one long gray mass that watched me, goaded me, and laughed at me as I traversed the final stretch. I tried to ignore them, even as some of them aspired to greater dimensions and greater features, elementary faces struggling to transcend this wall that was suddenly like a portal. But it wasn't. It was my goddamn apartment hallway and nothing else.

Nothing else.

I heard voices from my apartment. Guests had arrived. I reached the door and set down the container and stopped—how could I tell them this? How could I start the new millennium by subjecting myself to such an embarrassing spectacle? I would blame it on the mushrooms, I decided. Yes. They had kicked my brain off its axis, thrown me for a loop. And I'd try to lateral the laughs to Mikhailov. Or his friend who'd made the cookies. Anyone.

I went in. Heads turned, though not as many as I expected.

"Patman!" said a med school buddy of mine named Devon. "You okay? You look—wild. Exhausted."

"He's been partying somewhere else first!" quipped another friend, Anna, a writer and ex-fling. "That Benedict Arnold!"

Shaking my head and laughing (mostly at myself), I brought the container in and threw a universal greeting to every face in the room as I made a beeline for the couch and collapsed next to a man named Alex, one of Mikhailov's friends. He smiled at me and sipped a glass of vodka.

As Mikhailov diligently began unpacking the container, he said, "You carry this from store?"

"I did," I said. "Thought I'd get a workout."

"Jesus," said Devon. "Hope you lifted with your legs."

"I would've been fine, too," I said, pointing, "had I not accidentally taken one of those damn cookies."

Several murmurs of "What cookies?" ricocheted from tongue to tongue. Mikhailov looked at me quizzically. "Cookies?"

"The chocolate chip!" I said. "Those were the mushroom cookies you said you got from your friend, right?"

"Ohh." Comprehension washed over his big round face and I felt validated, though it was very short-lived. "No, no, I never get them. Serge bring them later."

I could feel blood make funny movements in my veins. I wasn't sure what to say and felt no compulsion to press the issue, especially with everyone looking at me. From every one of my vitals grew the coarse bristles of humiliation. I wanted to jump out of my skin, scamper away like some runaway ghost.

Gratefully, the visions had passed.

"Throw me a drink," I said.

Much of the party thereafter was a blur, though a memorable blur. Particularly I remember a prominent, underlying emotion—appreciation. Appreciation for this small world of mine, these friends. It was an intimate vessel on dark seas, the waters of which lashed its every side, without buffer. We may often think we're on an earthly cruise ship drifting on this Sea of Mystery, but we're actually just floating in it, partially submerged and vulnerable, kicking and stroking along. Hell, we *are* it.

This small world of mine was a fragile one, a temporary one, but I was there in it, and that night I somehow knew that better than any other. Fundamentally, we're all one shade of ignorance, a family of unknowing, and can take comfort in little else beyond another's presence.

At midnight, we joined the millions on this coast watching and chanting with the rerun of the Times Square celebration.

"Ten—Nine—Eight—Seven—Six—"

Anna put her arm around my shoulder, touched her drink with mine. "So Soon-to-be-Doctor, what's going to happen these next thousand years?"

I shrugged. The doorbell rang.

"*Three—Two —One—Happy New Year!*" Added by most everyone, "And Millennium!"

With a blower jutting from his mouth, Mikhailov went to get the door. There was an excited, rapid-fire exchange of Russian, and a slim man walked in carrying a covered plate. I picked up his name was Serge. In English he apologized for being late, and Mikhailov teased him further in Russian.

Serge set his plate next to the cookie dish I'd taken from earlier, which was now a wasteland of crumbs. As far I know, no one had an inkling of the issues I'd had after eating them.

Mikhailov gestured, mostly looking at me. "Cookies come!"

I waved him off. "No, no."

She & He

Bang.

She heard the shot from half a block away, and knew— somewhere in the world below—that the unexpected had taken place.

The late afternoon saw her carry in two overweight grocery bags, staggering through the small apartment door in an almost drunken manner. A box of cookies hit the floor with a sharp cardboard *thwack*. As usual, he ignored her, choosing to remain by the window with the rifle.

"How was work today, dear?" he asked with stale interest.

"Oh, same ol', same ol', you know how it is." She piled the bags on the kitchen counter. "That toothpaste you like was finally on sale. Got the last one, too."

He didn't say anything, only aimed his gun.

Bang.

She began laying out the groceries, lining them up in the order they were to be slotted into the refrigerator. The three cartons of eggs went first, piled atop one another, followed by the two juice jugs, orange for her and apple for him. She saw his taste for apple juice as a childish idiosyncrasy, not fully understanding how someone so old could have such a

13

juvenile sweet tooth. Yet he was the first to admit that, in many ways, he was and always had been a child, often at odds with responsibility or discipline regarding anything but his own work.

"Dammit, can't you clean up your mess in here?" she said, weaving her way around the unkempt heap of dishes in the sink. "Just toss them in the dishwasher. I've got enough to do at work without having to come home and clean your messes."

"Who do you think makes the messes you clean at work?" he muttered, his laser focus unbroken.

"Exactly," she replied. "So can't you keep the apartment somewhat tidy, for my sake?"

He swerved the gun left and pulled the trigger. *Bang*— and the chest of a business executive named Martin Brooks became an impenetrable knot. The poor man buckled to the pavement of a New York street corner, life leaving him in wheezy, gasping breaths.

"A heart attack is just nature's sniper shot," he mused aloud, watching the reactions of people around Brooks.

"Mr. Brooks was getting a raise tomorrow," she said, irritated. "I was planning on him moving upstate with his family in the next year or so."

"Shit happens, dear."

Uneasy silence gripped the next few minutes. The world below sat waiting, rotating nervously as it sensed his trigger-happiness. From their apartment window they could see the vast green jigsaw pieces, separated over miles of water, all aged with the rust of humanity. It needed constant spit shining, from both of them. He saw people as they saw ants, so plentiful and insignificant, yet he knew his job was beneficial to them. Baby Mankind was taking its first steps, after all—it needed to trip once in a while, to fall, if it was ever going to stand on its own.

In another *bang*, the land beneath the city of Tokyo shuddered like a wet dog trying to dry itself.

She closed the refrigerator door and sighed. "Guess I'll have to put in overtime tomorrow. I hate making sense of disasters."

"Hey," he said, looking at her for the first time since she'd walked in. "You get paid more than I do, live with it. Plus, I was about due for another earthquake."

He raised his gun again, this time angling it towards a long passenger train that rumbled its way across the English countryside. He peered through the sight, then hesitated, as though in doubt, and for a fleeting moment she saw umbrage, or perhaps forlorn hope, in his face—a pain that survived on crumbs of remorse.

But she knew that wouldn't stop him. He wasn't a bad guy by any stretch of the imagination, just a guy obligated to do his job, as she was with hers. And a vacation for either one was, quite frankly, inconceivable. The very balance of the Whole would be tipped, the universe lopsided and brain-damaged. The threads of perception stitching every dimension together would tear and fray like discarded strands of dental floss.

He was he. She was she.

The rifle's crosshairs found the train and kissed it from

afar. His fingers rested on the trigger, giddy and eager. She could feel his pulsating energy, the energy that tipped dominoes, flapped butterfly wings, ignited storms.

Bang.

Rummages in the Room

I

"Am I the first one that's going to have to say it?" Curtis said to his wife Lani, now driving them up the curved mountain road.

"Say what?"

"Am I the only one somewhat frightened by the prospect of spending a long weekend with them? In the same cabin?"

Lani shook her head, her *What am I going to do with you?* expression one Curtis had seen aplenty, and, though he hadn't told her so, found among the most attractive. "You're just now bringing this up? And come on, you're not frightened, are you?"

"Maybe not frightened—"

"That's your usual hyperbole coming out."

"My usual. Right. Thanks."

"I know we've had our recent... squabbles with them, but I still love Jan. I've loved her for two decades. And short of her sleeping with you, I don't see any reason why I shouldn't love her the next two."

Lani was curiously quiet about Dean. Since Dean and Jan

had married, and since their wives were such longtime friends, Curtis had been cornered into friendship with the man, the "couple friendship" superseding the individual one. To a certain degree, Curtis had grown to enjoy his time with Dean, despite tense political differences.

This was an election year, however. What's more, it was a presidential election year. The national juices were already bubbling in the heat, sure to reach boil in a few months. Recent efforts by Curtis to avoid related topics with Dean had, not a week ago, collapsed against the subject of Republican candidate Jim Downs, a former senator from Lani's home state of Wisconsin. Curtis considered Downs a welcome, refreshingly acceptable addition to the other side of the aisle. Dean, ever the contrarian, thought Downs too liberal for a serious conservative contender.

"He's corrupting Jan, you realize," said Curtis. This time he caught himself. "Right, right, I know. Corrupting! Ever the exaggerator. But you haven't noticed that?"

"They assimilate, adapt, like any couple," Lani said. "But Jan always holds her own. And she's always been moderate. She voted Republican last election."

The subject remained dormant for the rest of the trip. Curtis thought it sure to thrive in quick glances, elbow jabs and closed-door back-and-forths. He resolved, as he had before, to make light of it for himself, to move the political hot button from his heart to his funny bone, where things were not nearly as infuriating as they were amusing, if occasionally irritating.

Laugh about it, a colleague named May in the neighboring classroom had told him. *You'll keep years on your life*. Curtis had nodded at the sage advice when May, in turning to leave, had added, *You can live to see it all go to hell.*

Such apocalyptic notions, whether jokey or serious, had over the last few years cultivated in Curtis a gloominess that was foreign to his character. Like a thrown gas canister, the pessimism had begun as a thread of smoke but had since seeped across the outer layers of his mind, tainting words and memory and opinion, clouding his eyes, where Lani, speaking playfully but observing regretfully, said it was "pretty visible." She worried about the "vibe" he might be sending to his students, who were teenagers and needed no excuse for cynicism. She also worried, as he sometimes did, that it had accounted for the slight decline in their social life, one of the reasons Lani hung tight to Jan.

They entered a passage flanked by the green imperialism of mountain pines. Curtis occupied himself with the foreverness of the passing woods. Unlike fellow environmentalists with noble—often quixotic—schemes of "saving it all," his environmentalism derived more from humility than maternal protection. The planet would see us off laughing. Out here, in the rugged expanse of nature, all buttons hot or cold led to the funny bone, to a place of detached amusement, to enviable indifference.

***

On seeing the cabin, Curtis was struck with a strange uneasiness. The place, after all, was a beautiful, two-story house with a deck, a grill area, and large airy windows. At the same primal level as this odd fear stirred equally baseless relief that he and Lani would, after all, not be here alone.

"This is the kind of place I'd like to live in someday," Lani said, clearly unaffected by whatever it was that niggled Curtis. "Wonder what these cabins go for."

Lani's cell phone rang. She answered it and spoke for only a moment.

"That was Jan," she said. "She and Dean are running late. They might get here tonight, or stop on the way and come in the morning."

Having promised themselves minimal packing this time, they were able to carry everything they'd brought for the weekend in one schlep. Approaching the front door, they heard voices. Inside.

Lani frowned. "Sounds like the TV's on."

She unlocked the door and they went in. Curtis felt a sting of cowardice allowing his wife first entrance.

"Hello?" Lani called.

No reply, save for the tube's colorful claims to *Call right now!*

Curtis waited until the commercial with the ab-crunching woman was over, then turned it off.

"Weird," he said. "You think the cleaners left it on?"

Lani shrugged and moved off towards the staircase. "I'm putting my stuff away."

Curtis envied his easygoing wife. She reserved attention for worthwhile things, not every random oddity. The television being on had only inflamed his prodigious (and, admittedly, neurotic) anxiety about this place. It was a precursor. A handful of times he'd encountered otherwise ordinary things, unexpected or out of place, that seemed harbingers of larger, unrelated abnormalities to come.

"Holy Godmother!" Lani cried.

Curtis rushed to the bottom of the stairs. "What is it?"

"Come up here now!" she said. "The size of this bedroom—huge!"

***

His phone's alarm clock went off quietly, waking only him. Lani, still asleep, just groaned and shifted slightly. Curtis slipped from the sheets and peeled back the curtain to see the morning outside so crisp and still. He did his routine sit-ups then left the bedroom, gently clicking the door closed behind him, and went to the kitchen where he found Dean up and making coffee.

Dean grinned. "Fellow morning buff."

"When did you guys get in?" Curtis asked. "Didn't hear you."

Dean chuckled. "That's good. We didn't want you to hear us. We got in late because Jan realized halfway here that she forgot her hiking poles. She swears by those things—she's got that sciatica."

Curtis nodded. "I'm glad you guys got here safe."

He went to the large living room windowpane. The forest was at its most primeval in the early morning, as if participating in some mass prayer or meditation all led by the chants of doves. The shadows kept their secrets until the sun rummaged through and revealed them.

Steaming cup of joe in his hand and the paper in the

other, Dean sat at the kitchen table. "How's the sculpting?"

Curtis was surprised by the inquiry. "It's on standby at the moment. I've just been busy with school. But I want to finish my current piece by the end of the month."

"Well, let us know," Dean said, unfolding the paper. "Jan keeps saying we need some 'decorative accent' for the dining room."

From there the first day passed well enough. The couples had brunch together in the village and stocked up on groceries. When they returned in the afternoon, Dean and Jan took a nap to recharge from their late-night arrival, during which Curtis, continuing a daily habit since a cholesterol scare, took a long walk through the hills. Half a mile in, he encountered a split path, the left sloping down, the right sloping up.

Had he taken the left path that afternoon, there might've been nothing further to tell.

They had dinner and played *Trivial Pursuit*, the first round of which was couple against couple, then the men against the women. During the latter game Curtis felt a heartening sense of camaraderie with Dean, which helped quell much of the unease that had begun the trip.

The evening ended around the late television news. Clutching cups of hot tea, Lani and Jan spoke amongst themselves as Curtis and Dean sat watching the glossy anchors impart the day's headlines. A segment came up about Jim Downs's latest speech in Florida, and Dean leaned over.

"You know I meant to tell you—I picked up Downs's biography," he said. "A few days ago."

"Hm," said Curtis. "That's the one that just came out?"

"Couple weeks ago, yeah. *Down Country* it's called. I always read the bios of the big candidates. See what we might be in for."

A pause.

"I think he's a lot more conservative than you might think," said Dean. "It's come to make me feel better."

"So then…a lot of his more left-leaning policies he talks about are empty promises designed to lull the other side," Curtis said. "That's still sleazy no matter how you slice it."

"That's been the game for centuries," said Dean. "We all vote on ideas, notions. Things lighter than air."

"How do you know he isn't just pandering to your side?"

Dean smiled. Lani and Jan stood up, empty cups dangling from their fingers.

"We're hittin' the hay," Lani said.

"Good idea," said Curtis. "I'll join."

"You coming, Dean?" Jan said.

Dean remained in his seat, eyes ahead. "Be there in a minute."

II

The two men were, again, the first awake the next morning, and again Dean came out before Curtis.

Dean sat in the kitchen with a dreamy, disconnected look, shifting eyes from the window to the book in his lap, which Curtis saw was *Down Country*. The newspaper lay on the table, rumpled and read.

"Morning," said Curtis, pouring himself coffee. "Thanks again for brewing."

"No problem."

Several moments passed. Curtis could almost feel the heat of Dean's eagerness to engage him on headlines and topics, to exploit their temporary solitude. Men were like that—the war impulse operated in everything from battlefields to board games to conversations. But he also sensed Dean might be too hesitant to make the first move.

He asked instead if Dean wanted to accompany him on his early walk.

The man's expression was a strange combination of dreamy disconnection and hardened business.

"Sure," said Dean. "Let me get my shoes."

***

They took the same route Curtis had the previous day. Neither of them spoke much; Curtis suspected this bothered his companion more than it bothered him. He liked the dawn hour for its quiet, for its lack of people and activity. It was the only time he could hear in full the whispers of the world's real personality.

When the men did speak, it was in short, trivial bursts, remarks on the pine-cool smell of the air, the color of the sky, the freshness of the forest.

Soon, they came to the divergent paths.

"Well," Dean said neutrally, "which way?"

"I took the right path yesterday," Curtis said. "Let's see what's on the left."

He was afraid Dean might spin some political joke, but the man just took a deep breath and said, "Left it is."

They walked in silence for another ten minutes. The path quickly degraded, losing its definition as grasses, weeds, and trees encroached, narrowing the path more and more. No signs or cabins stood in this stretch—they were entering a wild stretch. Curtis's stomach tightened.

Dean stopped and pointed. "What is that?"

He couldn't see anything, and so stood behind Dean and followed his finger through the wooded striations to a sliver of what looked like a gray stone resting not far into the forest.

"Looks like it could be an altar," Dean said with schoolyard fancy. "Or tombstone."

They went farther. The trail didn't loop. In fact, the last of its waning identity became lost in the green.

From another vantage point, the men could see more of the gray structure, which was square and smooth, like a boxy thundercloud. There was an eeriness about it—maybe it *was* a mausoleum, or something.

"We should check it out," Dean said.

"Why?" The question, though voiced moderately to his companion, was bellowed inwardly as Curtis also knew the inexplicable pull of this place, whatever it was.

"Because it's off the beaten path," Dean said. "And it doesn't look too brambly getting there."

"What about ticks?"

Dean started off, leaving the question unanswered. Curtis soon followed. Earth crunched and popped beneath his soles, the fine-needled fingers of pine brushing his open skin like curiously invasive spectators. In here the land became the sky, the ink-blotted canopy masking the young light of the morning.

When the building was in full view, it almost seemed a mirage. In the wildly ruffled, erratic freedom of the forest, the thing stood as a monument to absolute order, to mathematical precision, to neat and fine intention.

And yet its incongruity was the sole source of its perceived strength. A windowless box, it looked like a bunker or a bomb shelter, or, comically enough, a large present left by Christmas pines. Its surface, while gray, was not rugged brick or stucco or concrete. Nor was it metal. It was too smooth and soft. Almost like gray skin.

Approaching closer only muddled the problem further. The box rested on a circular patch of dried yellow grass. The men began walking around it, noticing other things—or lack of things. No pipes or propane tank. No sign of use or habitation. No stains or markings on the faintly glistening walls.

Reaching the other side, they found a door. By most accounts it looked normal, made of metal with a rusted brass knob and two rectangular panes of glass that, to Curtis, resembled a pair of dark, foggy eyes.

Having avoided its radius of yellow grass, Curtis took the first cautious step onto it, closer to the door. A thought struck him.

"Hand me a rock," he said to Dean.

Dean scanned the area, then retrieved a palm-sized stone and handed it to Curtis, who hurled it at the door. It hit with a dead, metallic *thunk*. They waited. No one came out. Nothing stirred. The door didn't budge.

"Hello?" Curtis cried.

"Maybe they're asleep."

Of course, it was likely empty, or abandoned. There weren't any trucks or cars or driveways around. But it was unshakable, the idea that this room was somehow occupied. There was a presence here.

"Let's just try the door," Dean said.

Curtis wanted to stop him but couldn't, and watched as Dean went up to it and touched the knob and turned it.

The door opened—revealing an utter mess. Piles of papers, books, newspapers, more papers. There were paintings too, some of which were hung; others were scattered like file separators among the paper landfill. The smell reminded him of a public restroom, some mix of cleaning agents and crap.

"Christ," muttered Dean. "Someone has a hoarding problem."

There didn't appear to be anyone here, though Curtis still sensed a presence. This feeling went unvoiced but undeniably shared, as both men moved cautiously into the room, as if tingling with expectations of a surprise greeting.

"I don't think we should be here," Curtis said.

They were drawn to a mound of flesh-colored paper: a haystack of erotic imagery. Scantily-clad catalogues. The raw and the pornographic. Dean noticed something in the pile and peered closer. Curtis could tell he wanted to pick up the object of interest but refrained, likely out of revulsion.

The picture looked decades old, its color washed, its

subjects—at least the woman—sporting an old late-sixties hairstyle. Such a trivial feature, however, took a backseat to the rigorous throes of doggy-style intercourse in which she was engaged. The woman was by far the most visible, the man more blurred. Curtis realized the picture moved (*moved*?), like a hazy choppy animation.

"It's… moving," he said. He checked the door behind them. Could it be a trick of what little light was coming in?

"I'm noticing it," said Dean coolly. "I'm also noticing that that's Caroline Downs."

It took a moment for the name to catch up to Curtis. "Caroline Downs…"

"Jim Downs's wife."

Filling Dean's eyes in that moment was an unnerving wonder Curtis had never seen on someone's face, not in real life.

"Are you sure? What about these others?"

"I'm pretty damn sure. The biography I'm reading… there are pictures. New and old. This must be thirty years old, this picture…"

They explored further, soon relinquishing all prior hesitance at touching the images and papers. The erotic pile received the brunt of their initial focus, and as they sifted, perused, leered, they uncovered what must have been thousands of different women's faces, age-wise all within a decade of one another. Dean noticed that, while many of the pictures of Caroline Downs were of a younger woman, only a handful showed her as she was now—as Curtis and Dean and the rest of the nation had come to know her.

Thoughts rampant and words scarce, the men rarely opened their mouths, and when they did the subject fluctuated from the trivial ("Christ, look at this one") to solemn notions of someone trying to blackmail Downs. Beneath their exchanges, however, lay a prickly sense of otherness, minor enough to deny but which held the men in a kind of loopy timelessness.

As they explored, Curtis noticed a pattern. When he didn't focus on any one item, the entire pile melded into thousands of indistinct forms. Concentrating on one, however, tended to alert him to a number of similar or related pictures, either because of similar positions or because they were of the same woman.

The men began pocketing some of the erotic images. Neither said anything to the other, though Curtis noticed he was prone to discretion more than Dean, whose goofy-grinned reap of the bounty was unapologetically brazen.

"This is unbelievable," Dean said. "Who has an unlocked shack of private pictures in the woods? We've got to let people know about this. Or maybe just Downs's people."

Curtis nodded.

"We should see what we want to take first," Dean went on. "You think he'll notice if we do? I mean, how could anyone keep track of this stuff?"

"Why should we take anything?" Curtis said. "We shouldn't be *in* here."

"Don't give me sermons," Dean said. "You nicked at three of those pictures."

"None of this makes any sense," he said, blowing past

Dean's comment. "A presidential candidate leaves a pile of private, damnable stuff in the middle of the wilderness—across the country."

Dean shrugged. "I mean, what's here is here."

How can he be so *flippant* about this? Curtis thought. But part of him knew: it was that persistent, puzzling sense of belonging.

They spent another half-hour exploring.

"I think that's a portrait of his grandmother," said Dean, indicating one of the few pictures hung on the wall. "He credits his grandmother with his desire to run for office. Change the world. Says he wants to bring everyone else the inspiration she brought him."

Next to the pile of pornography was a stack of elementary school assignments, reports, lessons, some creased and browning with age, most scarred with the smeared loopy printing of an eager child. To his surprise, Curtis noticed one childhood reading exercise he himself had done as a kid, which had helped his reading tremendously. The coincidence was significant—not three weeks ago he'd tried to find a reprint for his colleague, June Thatcher, the special education teacher at his school. The effort had proven futile, so he'd tried to recreate it. Now it was here, though adorned with scribbles.

The name atop each paper, mostly written in pencil but some crayon, said *James Downs*.

"Yeah," said Dean, when he saw the pages. "He started going only by Jim when he ran for Senate, to sound more homegrown American, less European."

"What the hell *is* all this?" Curtis cried.

"I don't know," said Dean, still mostly dealing with the sexual pictures. "But I just stumbled upon what looks like a little college experimentation."

***

"That was quite a walk," Jan said, holding the front door open as the two men returned, stomping up the porch steps. "We thought maybe a bear had gotten you."

"Or Bigfoot!" Lani called from the steaming kitchen.

"That smell's really good," Curtis said. "Potato pancakes?"

Jan nodded. "And real pancakes. Your wife got the breakfast bug this morning."

"Wonderful," said Dean. He pecked his wife on the lips and moved quickly towards the stairs. "I'll be right down. Just going to take a shower."

Curtis followed. "Same here."

"Don't take too long!" Lani called. "It'll probably be ready in another ten or fifteen minutes."

The men hurried up to the second floor, sharing brief knowing eye contact before adjourning to their rooms. Curtis removed the images from his pockets and looked at them. None moved. In fact they appeared even more washed out, the colors dry, the contours blurry. He decided to keep them on him, placing them in a zippered pocket of his cargo pants so as to eliminate any chance Lani might find them in a bag or a drawer.

Next he brought out the reading exercise he'd taken and studied it, reminiscing, perplexed, on just how it had come

31

to be in his hands, on what kind of bizarre journey it had taken from little James Downs's busy mitts long ago to his own here today.

He slipped the exercise into his suitcase. Then he disrobed and showered and joined the wives at breakfast. Dean arrived a few minutes later.

***

The men didn't speak much to one another that day, merely trading silent questions with a mixture of edgy excitement. In brief moments, Curtis thought Lani had perhaps picked up on this tension. He'd prepared his best performance to assure her everything was all right, but she said nothing and neither did Jan.

That Saturday evening, all four of them drove into town for dinner. They chose a homey bar and grill, where they sat within audible range of the television now running sports wrap-up. While they sipped their drinks, one of the bar patrons asked for the channel to be changed.

Curtis felt a nudge. It was Dean. He turned and glanced at the television, where the blonde reporter stood before a milling crowd of signs and colors.

"An awkward moment for Senator Downs today," said the reporter, "at a speech in Florida. Downs approached the podium and looked like a deer in the headlights, confused as to what to do. He excused himself and asked to be taken to the hospital. No further information has since been released on what exactly might be wrong."

They cut to a witness from the audience, a pale mustached

man clutching a *Down for Downs!* sign (a response to the opponents' *Down with Downs* signs), who, while casting furtive glances everywhere but the camera, remarked, "It was weird. He just stood there, totally blank, looking at his notes or speech or whatever, then rushed off. I hope he's okay. It was like stage fright. I thought for a second he'd forgotten how to read."

III

Thankfully, Jim Downs had not forgotten how to read—at least not entirely.

Doctors attributed the baffling lapse first to a possible stroke, then migraine, and with each negated possibility the theories and terms grew humbler and vaguer, culminating in either a "neurological event" or a "fugue."

The incident set pundits' lips flapping about the man's physical and mental fitness for office. Some were thoughtful, prodding the candidate to seriously reconsider his bid for the good of himself and the nation. Others were less kind: *What kind of Commander-in-Chief gets stage fright?*

Sunday afternoon saw that weekend's last visit to the room. For the two men it was hardly even discussed aloud—they were caught in a steady undertow, enhanced by growing notions of what this place was.

With rising guilt, Curtis picked up and read pieces from Dean's copy of *Down Country*. Some of its passages startled him for their candidness.

"I was actually quite an anxious child, a shy child," said

one passage. "Moving through the streets of my Pittsburgh neighborhood or down the corridors of school I'd always feel quite vulnerable, like a lamb in the wilderness. I felt suffocated by the expectations of others, and that everyone was somehow ready to pounce on me. My nerves buzzed like backyard noise. But they were all silenced when we'd visit my grandparents in their coastal home in Maine, where I would watch the waves roll ashore, and stare at the horizon and feel calm and free, and at peace."

"I'm putting these things back," said Curtis, referring to the erotic images and reading exercise. They were walking through the woods. "It's not right. And these… pictures are fading."

Dean studied him. "You think the same thing I do, don't you?"

"What's that?"

"That somehow we were responsible for his little episode yesterday."

"That's… I don't know. Impossible."

"I noticed some things in there that seem to contradict some of what his biography says," said Dean. "I want to scrounge some more."

"And what do you plan to do?" Curtis brought out one of the fading photos from his pocket, its content blurred. "Apparently these things don't keep, whatever they are."

Dean said nothing as they approached the room and went inside. Curtis moved to the areas he'd combed prior and deposited the pictures and the reading exercise.

After several moments, both men were brought to attention by chirping noise behind them.

Sitting at the threshold, quivering with energy, was a plump squirrel. It scampered into the room, streaking like a furry little missile around the heap of materials, bounding and tearing and ruffling everything.

Dean went after it first, trying to maneuver with comparably clunky agility, but hopelessly outpaced and out-turned. Curtis took up the slack and in wayward zigzagging motions attempted to drive the chittering rodent back to the door, in the process disarraying some of the images himself.

"Get it out of here!" Dean cried.

Eventually the squirrel left, bolting out the door and back to the cooling forest, where it was lost in weeds and brush.

***

Both men avoided the news and newspaper when they returned to the cabin. Logging onto the internet, they only checked email. Curtis ignored the chimes of daily news alerts to his cell, putting the phone on silent after Lani looked at him, surprised he wasn't his usual Pavlovian self in opening it every time it sounded.

When the news did come it was Jan who broke it, during another game of *Trivial Pursuit*.

"You hear Jim Downs had a seizure earlier?"

Curtis and Dean looked at one another.

"Really?" Lani said. "Oh my God."

"I know. I wasn't sure I wanted to bring it up, lest I launch these two guys into another political spitting match." She pointed at Curtis and Dean. "But it seemed neither of you had heard."

"I didn't, no," Dean said.

Curtis shook his head. "No… what happened?"

"He was getting a burger at some famous local burger stand in Boston and collapsed. They rushed him off. I think he's okay. Sounded like a freak thing."

Dean sighed. "He's gonna take a nosedive for this."

"Yeah, well, it's definitely put his base on edge. And you know a lot of them aren't too fond of his VP pick, either."

The men were quiet, Curtis distracted to the point where Lani, his partner that round, punched him playfully a few times to, as she would say, "hammer him back to Earth."

Jan read an entertainment question.

"In what show did Rod Serling introduce stories from a series of paintings?"

"Oh, that's an easy one," Dean said.

"Crap," Lani said. "It wasn't *The Twilight Zone*, obviously. Argh! Do you know this one, Curt? It's on the tip of my tongue."

Curtis shook his head. "I've forgotten, too."

How could this happen? How was this even a conceivable, let alone possible, thing? If his and Dean's theories about the room were accurate, then not only did it defy all human understanding, but also, as far as Curtis was concerned, it defied nature's understanding of itself, if such a statement could at all be logically made.

Much of Curtis still vied for the explanation of coincidence, certain these anomalies in the news just happened to somehow correlate with his and Dean's exploratory rummaging. But, if true, how would it function?

Were certain parts of the room correlated to certain parts of the brain? How in God's name would that work?

It wouldn't. Because what you're thinking is beyond insanity.

"*Night Gallery!*" Lani shouted, slapping the table in triumph. "That was it!"

Yet there were those times, those rare times, when insanity proved the only voice of reason in the room.

***

Because of standardized testing, the next month saw a dip in Curtis' school responsibilities. He resumed his sculpting, finally finishing off a new piece half a year in the making. Standing three feet high, the new work was part of what he dubbed his "ocean canon," a swirling composition of a breaching whale beneath which a calf looked on in fascination.

Curtis brought Lani in and showed her. Her smile looked forced.

"You can't stand it," he said.

Lani struck his arm. "The chronic exaggerator. How could I not stand it? I mean, the technique is always good. You're a natural. But I still like *Tides* the best."

Curtis smirked. *Tides* had been done years ago, the first of his ocean motif and probably one of his more abstract installments: swirling waves, fixed in clay, crashing upon some forever-unseen shore. "Something almost equine about it," one friend had commented, "like a stampede of horses, but soothing." A younger colleague had said it made him want to go to the bathroom.

Lani crossed her arms. "I still want to put *Tides* out. But

37

I know you hate it and you hate me for liking it so I won't force it. As I just said, forcing it never does any good."

"I don't hate you for liking it," Curtis said, putting his arm around her shoulder and squeezing. "Now you're the exaggerator."

"Well, living with you as I do," she said, "it was bound to happen."

***

While grading papers during a morning test session, Curtis's phone buzzed with a text message.

It was from Dean.

We should go back to the room

Curtis didn't respond, not until the break period when his classroom was clear.

He called Dean.

"Why do you want to go back?" he said.

"We have to fix what happened. Whatever happened when that squirrel came in and we chased it. Something happened to him."

Although he'd tried not to follow too much the political game unfolding, avoiding news entirely was impossible. Curtis mused on the recent reports of Downs: notions of early dementia or brain damage, spurred by rumors of his newfound difficulty in reading or sounding out certain words or syllables (this made Curtis wonder if he'd needed to put the reading exercise back in the exact spot and position as before, though he couldn't be sure what those were), and a sudden plague of random seizures, the first of which Downs had described as "like having an animal pounce, claws out, on your brain."

"How are we going to do this?" Curtis said. "Fix it. I mean."

A pause. "We'll figure it out. We have a responsibility to figure it out."

Behind Dean's words, Curtis sensed a restrained eagerness.

"Why is it you really want to go, Dean?"

"I just told you."

You shouldn't go back there, Curtis thought. *But... but...*

But if this is what you think... did you really think you weren't going back?

"Dean, I'm thinking—"

"If you're thinking like me," Dean cut in, "we need to go back there. We need to see more."

"See more?"

"Add more, you know."

"Why?" Curtis said.

"Because," Dean said through an audible smile, "we have a candidate to make."

IV

The actual system of all these pictures—these memories—utterly confounded Curtis. Was this the way his own mind organized everything, this method-in-madness? And everyone else's? His students? Lani? Einstein? Where could one find the pervasive intelligence that maintained this order as assuredly as it saw to the order of trillions of other cells in all the organs of the body? Was the clueless self, the "soul," a curious tourist in classified territory, kept in disjointed, unknowing darkness? Certainly it had none of the body's mad genius.

Curtis voiced these thoughts as Dean drove them back to the forest.

"How is this supposed to work?" he asked. "How are we to know what we're doing and whether it's working or not while we're… in there?"

"We'll experiment. It's like your sculpting. Scrape, clump, refine, chisel, whatever you do."

"And while we do all that, Jim Downs has a stroke and pisses his pants in front of a massive crowd."

Dean said nothing. Given the persistence of his smile, Curtis wasn't altogether sure he'd heard him.

"Dean," he said.

A short pause. "What?"

"It's not fucking sculpting," Curtis said. "On a sculpture, I know what part is what. I know the layout. What we have here is a trash-heap of… of…."

"Memories?"

"Yes. Memories. Your plan might make sense, I mean, whatever sense can be salvaged from this, if we had a legend or boxes and cabinets labeled… I don't know… guilt or conscience or anger or something… you know what I mean."

"Okay. So?"

"The supreme make-up of someone is their memory. The memories are *every*thing. How can we possibly know what combination of removing and adding of certain memories

40

will result in what we want? Or fix what's wrong now? And these memories are fragmented. They're snapshots of days and nights and people and things. To remove one image would not be enough, not if we wanted to destroy the whole memory. And lastly, we don't know the significance of each picture. How important is one section of a memory versus another? Will removal of one have a ripple effect?"

"There's an order," said Dean. "The people close to him are framed, or on the wall. The memories significant to him are vivid and… well, they move, some of them do anyway, and you saw it—the piles are grouped by association and connection—"

"But, again," Curtis cut in. A thousand possible follow-ups bombarded him, but all he said was, "Who does brain surgery on a walking patient?"

Dean looked at him, expression flat. "We go while he's asleep."

***

They parked as near the trail split as possible, then took their flashlights and backpacks and climbed out. Dean went to the back and took out his .45 and Curtis, much to his chagrin, realized he'd never been so relieved to see a gun. Out here in the dark-soaked woods, a frail human amongst nocturnal prowlers, politics lost all edge.

"All set?"

Curtis sighed. "All set."

They walked, mostly silent, into the shadow-thickened forest, the moon granting a charitable drizzle of light. The woods smelled clean and cold.

"I don't even remember exactly where it is," Curtis said.

"It's halfway between the beginning of the trail and where it dissolves into the woods."

Every step for Curtis was another flared beat of paranoia. His pulse quickened. He worried each sound of theirs was another loud invitation for would-be creatures drawing closer and closer.

Dean stopped. "I think it's here." He stood still, shining his light against the impossible wall of wood, penetrating mere yards.

"You sure?"

He nodded slowly. "Let's go."

As with the first foray, Dean was the pioneer. Curtis hesitated, awaiting a blur of claws and screams, half-hoping for it, almost. But Dean pressed on, crunching twigs and leaves. With another deep inhale, Curtis entered the forest behind him and the bristly sarcophagi closed in on him, choking and wild and claustrophobic.

"I see it ahead," Dean announced.

Soon Curtis could also see the room, faintly aglow in a thin channel of moonlight. The glow was unsettling, too, as though a fine coat of radium paint had been applied.

Walking cautiously around to the front, their flashlights pooled upon the door—which was slightly ajar.

"Did we close it before?" Curtis asked.

"Pretty sure we did."

"Someone else is here."

"Hello?" Dean called.

No response.

Dean readied his pistol. The two men moved closer.

"Anyone in there? We're coming in."

With his foot, Dean pushed the door farther open. The flashlight cut into the small, square cosmos, revealing the usual piles of papers and pictures and moving across the eerie wall portraits until disclosing, in the center of the room, a quivering mass of flesh.

Curtis registered a naked man, squatting with his back to them.

"Excuse me," Dean said.

There was a delayed reaction in the man, who'd been sifting through several pictures. He turned to them like a raccoon caught scrounging through trash cans. He seemed wholly unaffected by the harsh light in his eyes, the glazed disconnection of which spoke more of the animal than the man, posing, for Curtis, the only brief obstacle to recognizing the person.

"It's Downs," he said.

Dean didn't reply.

"Mr. Downs…" Curtis stammered. "Are you okay? I'm… I'm sorry…"

"I'm reorganizing," said Downs, in a very congenial voice. "I'm reorganizing. It's the only time I have to do it."

"We're sorry to disturb you—"

Downs stood and turned. His movements were rubbery, somehow too fluid, as though he were a superimposed special effect.

"I hate almost everything in here," Downs said. "Hate it. Nothing is mine. It's someone *else's*. So where does that leave us? Nowhere. But we try to get somewhere, you know.

43

That's why I'm reorganizing."

The two men just stood there. Downs glanced around. Curtis imagined he might be freezing but somehow knew Downs, or this version of him, whatever it might be, was not touched too deeply by the world.

Suddenly the politician's face changed, opening in rage. He screamed and grabbed a pile of nearby pictures and threw them about the room. Limbs lashing and body shuddering, he hurled even more images, unleashing a blizzard of memories and dispersing them to far corners and crevices.

"We can't *stand* this, you know," Downs cried. "We need to find it. We need to strip away all of it, shuffle it all around because somewhere is us and somewhere is us buried here because it has to be, it *has* to be—"

He's having a nightmare, Curtis thought.

"Let's get out of here," Curtis said. "Now."

"Where am I?" Downs shouted, nearing scream-pitch. He chucked some pictures at Curtis and Dean. *"Where?"*

Dean started moving before Curtis did. In the whipping racquetball of his light, Curtis briefly noticed Jim Downs lurching after them. He knew, instinctively, that they'd be safe outside the room. Downs would not pursue them, there was no way, trapped as he was—trapped as anyone was in themselves—that he would give chase.

"Where am I?"

Fifty yards out, in the darkness of the forest, they heard him no more.

***

Jim Downs lost the election.

With almost callous haste, his name went out with the tide, washed into the choppy sea of media and political history. There was, of course, the anecdotal name-dropping that would cause one to remark, "That's right—whatever happened to him?" This was generally accompanied by a tiny tinge of guilt because they'd so quickly ceased to care about a person who, for nearly a year, had colored so many discussions and headlines.

Curtis Ambrose, of course, did not forget, best as he tried. Nor did Dean Bradford. They saw one another over the holidays and no mention of the room arose, though it hummed not far beneath their manners and their words.

As winter break approached, Lani approached Curtis and put her arms around his shoulders, her eyes lit with excitement—exaggerated excitement, thought Curtis.

"I have a job for you," she said.

He wasn't sure what to say, not these days. When they were dating such a statement usually meant she had an idea for a sculpture, and with a snicker she'd say, "I'm not like other muses, y'know—I don't just inspire. I *tell*."

"What's the job?" said Curtis.

"Over break," she said, biting her lip. "It would be fantastic if you cleaned the attic."

Curtis laughed.

"You don't have to do it all at once. You don't even have to clean all of it. Just some of the messier stuff. I went up there to get the Christmas things down and it's a landfill up there."

He began that day, starting with two large containers and three garbage bags for the smaller items. Thankfully, Lani asked not to be bothered with inquiries every five minutes about whether she wanted to keep something. "Unless you're absolutely sure I would want to keep something, don't let me know," Lani asked. "I haven't used much of any of that stuff in years and won't miss it. Ignorance is bliss, right?"

He worked for an hour before moving to the small trunk, where inside lay his more abstract piece *Tides*—that gush of ocean that had spilled out of him. Curtis wasn't sure how Lani could like it so much. And come to think of it, neither was she. But often things of certainty have little to no real, definable basis.

Then, he remembered something.

The following day, while Lani was out wine tasting with Jan, Curtis took his own solitary trip to the woods. *Tides* shuddered and bobbed in the passenger seat, as the vehicle climbed the mountain.

Moving through the streets of my Pittsburgh neighborhood or down the corridors of school I'd always feel quite vulnerable, like a lamb in the wilderness.

He parked in the same area as Dean had when they'd made their last visit. For several minutes he didn't move, instead peering down the trail, lost in ambiguous thought, the cooling engine ticking and the birds above crying and cawing.

I felt suffocated by the expectations of others, and that everyone was somehow ready to pounce on me.

He gathered the sculpture and made his way toward the room.

It wasn't visible, initially, and Curtis thought it might be gone. Looking closer, however, brought it into focus. Well aware of his solitude, he drew back his shoulders and headed into the woods towards the structure which, as he closed in, appeared as untouched, as undiscovered, as before.

And, just as before, the door opened with ease, creaking on its metal hinges.

No one there.

My nerves buzzed like backyard noise. But they were all silenced when we'd visit my grandparents in their coastal home in Maine, where I would watch the waves roll ashore, and stare at the horizon and feel calm and free, and at peace.

He hurried in and placed the sculpture in the middle of the room, unsure where in Downs's mind he might be leaving it, unsure of its relation to the other items. He knew it might be a risk but it was a necessary risk, a final effort to possibly, hopefully, set an inexplicable wrongness right.

At peace.

Curtis turned and left and, for the final time, closed the door.

Forces

If the world had ended, it had forgotten her.

Zoe White maneuvered against the cramped seating space, drenched in blackness.

Gone blind, I've gone blind. Just one of many thoughts flaring and fading like fireflies in her skull. She found her phone, its pale blue screen illuming the rest of the car's interior. All things beyond the windows, however, remained shut up in darkness.

Where am I?

She heard things—a motley of animal cries, mostly unrecognizable, though she could distinguish what were likely the birds and bugs. The longer Zoe listened, the more she appreciated the sheer volume of this orchestra, its thousands of throats, its symphony of uninhibited fertility. It sounded like a forest. A jungle.

Her cell phone returned no bars, no service.

Breath came in rasps, panic filling her like acid. Her heart drummed. Her ears buzzed with mounting fear. An unrecognizable scream tore from her own throat, struck the windows and went dead.

The unexpectedness of the situation, the sudden waking,

the darkness, had squandered her own thoughts, her own self. Memories pooled back into her mind. She had been in her car, yes. That was right. She had entered the final, final stretch of her journey to California. Where? To Los Angeles, yes. Yes, Naomi, her friend. Yes, her friend Naomi lived out here now, had for a couple years and Zoe was envious. Why? Why? Because… yes, because Naomi had just signed a contract with a big talent agent.

"I'm *so* excited," Naomi had oozed over the phone, as Zoe sat on her Texas porch blowing smoke toward the backyard of their many shared weekends and summers.

Naomi had continued, "I was just working at this café and this crazy-cute guy sits down next to me. He was all presumptuous and he just stared at me and I stared back and was like, 'Seriously?' I just didn't say that, of course… but he gave me his card and it's from this Hollywood agency, very reputable, super successful. And he thinks I have it."

"It?"

"Yeah! You know, *it*."

Zoe had been more than a little confused. Best as she knew, Naomi Lewis had still been immersed in her biochemistry scholarship at USC, mentioning the "Hollywood scene" only in quips about spotting celebrities "in daily street life" or in flippant replies to friends and family who would exploit every opportunity to jab her about it. But maybe Naomi had wanted to taste that world, after all—maybe academia had been the noble excuse to get closer to the cold warmth of neon star shine. Certainly they had talked about that when they were younger, never admitting to anyone, even to themselves, that such dreams were at all authentic.

Part of Naomi had not outgrown that dream, or fantasy, whatever it was. Neither had Zoe, really, if she had driven the two days from home to meet her friend out there. Not simply to visit her, as she'd constantly told herself and Mom and others, but to follow through on Naomi's offer to introduce her to her newfound agent, this shiny man-creature apparently named Tye Rhodes.

"Bring more pictures of yourself," Naomi had said. She had already shown Zoe's photo to this Mr. Rhodes—or Tye—who'd remarked, to Zoe's embarrassing titillation, "I can see that face on magazines. Get her out here!"

Two mornings later, Zoe had turned the ignition, a lone bulging duffel bag in the backseat. She had threaded the I-10 freeway, which supposedly ended in ocean. This new future would be bereft of all similarities to the old future, the current plan so long a begrudged certainty: the nursing route that, while admirable, did not *feed* her, did not *make* her.

Along the ride, Zoe had felt like she'd been entering another adolescence, one she could better control, appreciate. The heated newness of a second puberty, so many options and experiences awaiting her flesh. People would *know* her. People from home would know a newer, bigger her.

From the desert she had entered a mountainous pass, road signs declaring L.A.'s imminence. Over the hills the sun eased below an ocean that she would soon see in person. Dusk billowed across the sky. Headlights in frantic passing.

Caffeine the primary accelerant of her body and mind. And then the flanking mountains had parted, the martini glass of nighttime between them filling with the twinkling elixir of the city, the fiery wellspring of the world's dreams and legends there on her naked eye, no screen to buffer them, nothing between her and the promise of a new journey.

Zoe switched on the headlights. Only brush.

Somehow she'd veered off the road, into the woods. She hadn't crashed, though. The hood was intact. The dashboard as it was. No smoke or cracked glass or any sign of physical damage to herself.

Maybe I died, she thought. I died and now I'm stuck here.

She screamed again, dribbling off into prayer. For years now, God had been an errand to appease Mom, but His immense and unadulterated reality now returned to her. But if He had boxed her here in punishment, she would not allow it. She would show Him she was deserving of more. Let Him try and stop her any way He might.

She dug beneath the passenger's seat and brought out The Club, seldom used except when parking in areas that made her anxious. In preparing to strike the driver's side glass, she stopped. Maybe she was being rash. Could she open the door? Drive out of here? The latter didn't seem feasible. Heavy shrubbery entombed her. She noticed also huge tree trunks, rising like elephantine-legged guards.

How had she even gotten here?

She tried to start the engine, but turned out only a series of deadened clicks. Opening the door proved fruitless, too—the brush pressed against her, allowing only inches of leverage.

Raising The Club, she struck the window. Once. Twice. A crack. A third and it shattered. She kicked out the remaining shards. From her solitary luggage she slid on a long-sleeve shirt, then pressed the duffel bag against the imposing bushes as she pushed out like some large determined newborn from the thin gap in her car. She wanted to cry out more, but instinct told her otherwise.

Branches and ferns scraped her arms and torso. Hip-deep in the woods, she stopped. If this was Los Angeles, or near it, the air was much colder than expected. A breeze enveloped her like an icy shroud. Her breath smoked. It was colder than Texas. Wasn't California supposed to be warm? Last she remembered, it was spring.

There was also a different, less definable quality to the air, a sharpness, a kind of primal clarity.

Also, her rustling was not the only rustling.

Zoe stopped, angled in that awkward position. Listened. She couldn't see what moved in the woods. Whatever it was, though, was big. It crunched and snapped and ate. Its presence, perhaps progressively closer, stained the darkness with animal musk.

Zoe retreated to her car, cursing herself now for breaking the window. She couldn't stay here all night. She would freeze. Already her teeth chattered uncontrollably. Getting her blood moving in search of help might be the best thing to do.

But what's there?

The unseen beast continued around her car. More and more her ears appreciated its considerable size. She could hear rummaging, foraging disturbance in the trees above her, accompanied by regular, gastric grunts.

Breath came fast. She thought she might pass out and, trying to calm herself, withdrew like a turtle head into the protective shell of her car, where she continued listening and trying to watch.

Eventually, the noises of the great creature began to dim, the forest as still as it'd been when she'd awakened.

Zoe wasn't sure how long she stayed in the car, but it felt like hours.

***

"The world's two favorite pitches," Dad always said, "are screwballs and curveballs. On the odd occasion it throws a straight fastball, be sure you're ready with that bat."

And then her father had emerged from the deepest end of his own philosophy, his eyes trying to bite, to hold her with his perceived wisdom but trying, above all else, to focus through a Michelob haze.

"Actually," he had concluded, "just have your bat no matter what."

Zoe, in fact, enjoyed such plainspoken country wisdom—at the heart of it, mostly, were all the ideas that had been treated for thousands of years between book covers, usually in luxurious coats of language.

What kind of pitch is this, Dad? she thought, inching her

way through the brush. Her skin crackled with scrapes and pricks. She had found a small flashlight in the glove compartment, its batteries waning, and had chastised herself for not being better prepared with a stronger light.

I don't have my bat, Dad, she thought, tears rising in her. *I'm not prepared.*

For this.

For what?

Hopefully, the light would keep until she found the highway, or something at all man-made. So far no luck. Even just a beer can or a Taco Bell cup would suffice, for Christ's sake. Just *something* to indicate people actually came here.

She etched a prominent Z on each tree she passed, to help her find her way back to her car. She had also made sure to walk as straight as possible, and formed a pact with herself that, if she found nothing of value, or heard another unknown creature, she would return instantly.

Wafting back to her, like gaseous irony, came all the logical advice she had hurled at dumb movie characters. If this was a movie she was watching, what would her comfy, warm, snack-munching self say? She knew: *Stay in the car, you dolt. Go back.* How ridiculously dumb *was* this? But more than desperate seeking, more than the rationale of not sitting and freezing, terrible curiosity compelled her movement—where was she? What had happened? *How* had it happened? And why did this feel less and less like a curveball or screwball, and more like a fastball—a direct opportunity?

Then, through an opening in the canopy, light shone. She moved toward it.

The last of the trees parted, the moon hovering there. Not twenty yards ahead of her was an edge. She was on a cliff. She walked further out, her eyes filling with the great sprawl of the Pacific, moonlight a spectral island on its surface.

The ocean. Good. A reference point. A place from which to work backward, to orient.

Except the two coasts, extending north-south into midnight horizons, offered only more darkness. Far below, white-foamed waves curled to their end, exchanging hushed gossip with the shore. Their brief discoloration, vaguely perceptible, provided the only division between earth and sea. Where she expected a metropolis, where there was supposed to be trickling headlights, homes, buildings and lamps aglow, Pacific Palisades and Malibu and Santa Monica and all their fairy-land makeup, there was only more night.

The city was gone.

What the hell...

She noticed the sky, pulsing with stars and clouded with a spectacular Milky Way, a galactic show so impossibly and so profoundly crystallized that she assumed it was unreal, that she was hallucinating, or that somehow a doctored photograph had been wallpapered across the heavens.

From the brush far below issued an animal cry, one she recognized but would never have expected, not here. It was a familiar sound, like those she'd heard in zoos and in movies though this one was tinnier, angrier—more primordial, somehow. And it wasn't a cry so much as a trumpet.

A trumpet. Like an elephant's.

By the breakers far down the beach, a light went on. It began small and grew, the first star boring its way through an increasingly transparent earth. The light brightened, wavered, flickered.

Fire. A lone campfire around which moved faint shadows, bobbing upon the sand.

Slowly, Zoe made her way back to her car, her body racked by shivers. Curled up in five layers in the backseat, she barely slept. When she awoke at dawn, chilled and sickly but alive, she wasn't sure if she were grateful.

Nor did she know what to make of the strange, intense people surrounding her vehicle.

**

The moment she saw them, a dizzying exhaustion took her, her eyelids falling like curtains on what had to be a movie projected all around her. Zoe saw only men, mostly naked— one entirely—with bronzed skin and short-cropped black hair and Asiatic eyes. They carried long spears, and as she dipped once more into darkness she saw them come cautiously forward, though they did not seem threatened by her.

They know me, she thought, without understanding why. And then the world fell away, returning once again in another stroke of perception, a finger clearing a line in a fogged window, and she realized she was being taken downhill. To her right was the ocean, radiant with morning. Then more darkness, then a beachside village. Rustic. Nothing else. Wood huts and a stone campfire sighing smoke, and ruggedly-chiseled canoes and hanging meat and massive skins and furs. More eyes around her, many young. A pregnant woman.

She was taken inside one of the huts, where they laid her on soft skin. Two creased palms hovered over her and voices chanted, a shaky, elderly female voice predominant among them. Tingles in her bones. A sense of returning, of pieces reconstituting.

She blinked, and was fully conscious.

The other presences left, leaving only two at her bedside, a man and a woman, both old. Intuitively, Zoe knew them to be high-ranking, maybe the matriarch or patriarch of this village, this tribe, whatever they were. In hushed, extinct language they spoke to one another. There was a creaminess to the whole texture of their reality, a fluid and dreamy veneer.

When the woman left, the elderly man addressed her.

His eyes were ceremoniously forlorn, as though he had seen much hardship but knew also its virtue, and so would not relinquish a moment of it. The world had sketched remarkable topography on his face, and his voice was sullen and gravelly, as if originating from the very earth below, he the medium, the outlet of elemental wisdom.

Most incredibly, unlike the others she could understand him, and he her. While speaking different languages, communication was mysteriously not a problem. Their words passed through an unseen membrane, an ethereal translator that peeled away the breath, leaving only the meaning, utterly clear and universal.

"I don't know where I am," Zoe said. "Or why I'm here."

For a long while he studied her, then said, "You wouldn't

be here, if this wasn't the place you sought."

"No, I don't understand. I'm not seeking this. I'm not seeking to be lost—"

"Perhaps you were lost."

She looked at him. He continued.

"If one is so accustomed to being lost, they may not know when they have been found."

"I'm sorry—I'm sorry, I'm not supposed to *be* here—"

"The faces," said the elder. "Only the faces of the world change. Not the forces."

"What do you mean?"

"Take comfort," he said, picking up a clump of leaves, crunching them in his palm and sprinkling them over her body. "Only the faces have changed. You will grow to know past them."

Half of Zoe wanted to cry out of desperation. The other, echoing from a distance, knew what this man said, and that he spoke true.

***

From what she learned through the elder, the tribe referred to her as "the visitor," and assigned to her few of the customs or expectations of their own women, young or old. Zoe sensed their uncertainty about her even being human. Did they think she was a spirit? A god? An alien?

Not a god, she realized, or even a spirit—she realized they were not reverential, but more like landlords, or managers of a hostel, accustomed to seeing many such faces float in and out of their space.

Overall, the *de facto* decision seemed to be that she ought to remain in the village, with the women and children, but this was not enforced. One of the mothers—or, possibly grandmothers—taught her how to weave coiled baskets and twined-fiber blankets, and she marveled at the efficiency of the old woman's hands as they flipped and flew over her work. Zoe enjoyed the craft, finding it meditative.

By all personal accounts, she was the same person she had always been, even if memories of her old, or regular, life were mysteriously removed from her being. With effort, she could recall them, but they existed as if behind bubble glass, perceptible but distorted.

Her biggest question, which she knew the elder couldn't properly answer: When *am I?*

Had she transported to a future barren of any memory of civilization, her civilization? No. Growing intuition said that wasn't the case. She was seeing what it had been, hundreds, probably thousands of years before the first Anglo face, eons before anyone mad enough came along and decided the mountains could use massive white letters or mansions.

Increasingly, she knew herself becoming entranced, succumbing to a spiritual drowsiness. At fathoms deeper than intellect, she understood that she belonged here, that she had come here of her own accord.

***

It wasn't so much the culture but the atmosphere, the whole damn place, alleviated of so much weight of concrete and steel, of the noises and the messiness which had all been sucked from the air. Zoe remembered very little of the postcards and pictures she'd seen of Los Angeles' coastline, and her mind sometimes playfully projected onto this scene around her the buildings and the towns and the piers she thought were once—or would be—there.

Livelihood was simple, symbiotic, the tribe an assemblage of families. Every night they slept in the wooden huts, ears kissed by the sound of ceaseless waves, the salt-breezes fraying the campfire smoke. While uncertain of the exact season, the stubborn Southern California sun was just as reputed. During the day the children scampered in the sand, digging up crabs and finding insects, overseen by their mothers and aunts and elders. One of the boys, recently of age, was discouraged from such recreation, and ushered alongside other young men into the palm-lipped wilderness where they would learn to forage and to hunt. Despite her father's zest for it, Zoe had never hunted and so before had not understood it, but she understood it here, where every meal entailed a dangerous retreat, a rugged hike and a wildlife sightsee of the highest order. This was nature's cubicle, its lab, its stage, its worksite. They would gather berries and plants and haul the kills and collections back to the village and the food, so fresh, would awaken in her mouth taste buds long dormant, as if she'd enlivened a second tongue.

Zoe noticed they produced no art, at least no object with the conceit of art. All activities were patently practical. Zoe thought it sad, but soon wondered if *living* was not their art? Art, as she knew it, was a way of reconciling a wayward self with a natural self, a way of finding rhythm and meaning. But these people had rhythm. They had meaning.

Sometimes they would enter the sea, pushing canoes against the unwelcoming waves, then cross the bay towards the nearby island that in unknown centuries, if she remembered correctly, would be called Santa Catalina. Zoe would join them, and it was on one of these crossings, sitting centered in a canoe, bobbing on the sun-dappled sea, that a word entered her mind, a word that, well-worn, nonetheless had found significance, its true kin in the world of things.

Paradise, she thought.

The waters were shiny and jeweled. Zoe saw little of the larger marine creatures. Once, while in transit to Catalina, she thought she saw the shuddering silhouette of a giant shark. But it soon vanished. She had mentioned it later to the elder, who referred to it as the "Emperor of the Deep."

The islands were bearded with kelp forests, and full of multi-colored fish. Sometimes seals and sea lions zipped through, and sometimes the tribespeople would spear them, as well. They also caught the birds, the gulls and pelicans, and others she didn't know. Zoe disliked the blood and the death, but recognized it all as the rules of a game set down well before the first tooth or limb had sprung.

Come evening, they would often gather around the central fire, enshrouded in animal skin, as the elder told stories, his gestures and his words recalling vivid accounts of creation or the ancient world or the very creatures that dwelt in the darkness beyond the beach. Many tales involved the "golden death," the beast that stalked the hills, that rivaled their own hunting hand, and had been known to feed on their kind. By his description, and the doodle etched in sand, Zoe figured it a lion of some sort, a prehistoric cat.

The elder also told stories of what he called the "First People." Only he spoke of them, as if it were a subject too sacrosanct to be addressed by anyone lower or younger. But he spoke of how they had once flourished in these lands and these hills, how they had even carved their gods into the cliff faces, and how remnants of their once-great society could be found in the coves and caves deep in the canyons. To the tribe, these "First People" seemed a religion.

"You mean, there were people even before us?" Zoe asked the elder. The word "us" had come out naturally, unconsidered.

"Yes," the elder said. "Well before. The land resonates still with their presence."

Such people were not, it seemed, connected with the other tribes occupying more northerly territories, mention of whom tended to be discouraged. During a hunting excursion that Zoe had joined, one of the young men had pointed to the hills across the brush-choked basin, where campfire smoke unraveled into the sky. Although she could not understand his tongue, she understood that such regions were forbidden.

She bore witness to creatures previously glimpsed only as illustrations, fossils, or dead-eyed museum reconstructions. Families of woolly mammoths gathering about watering holes. Giant, hairy, equine-faced beasts—sloths, she would later recall—pressing their great bulk against heaven-groping trees. Herds of large, elk-like animals, sporting formidable antlers, swept across open plains. According to the elder, the tribe had resolved to kill only one mammoth—or "hair-tooth"—per year, at the summer solstice. "Their families are dying," he noted.

One of the younger hunters taught her how to craft a spear, stripping the wood, soaking it, splitting the end so that the ground stone could be hafted to it. Others had points made of ivory or antler. Zoe spent weeks practicing, poising and throwing, learning to enlist not only the hand and the eye but the entire body, of which the spear was an extendable limb.

She trained near the village, and more frequently accompanied their hunts, participating even in that year's mammoth hunt. The strategy involved calculated stages of division and conquest. One mammoth, a male adolescent, inevitably went astray and the tribe pursued it, unleashing their spears into its mountainous frame. The creature thrashed and bellowed, its cries weakening incrementally over the day-long ordeal. Two fellow hunters were nearly impaled or crushed.

Eventually, the mammoth collapsed, its spirit riding out its last great exhale. There was celebration, which turned solemn. Zoe just watched, torn by sadness and victory and a sense of futility. Such power extinguished. Where did it go?

***

The forest enclosed her. She followed the lightly-worn trails until they faded off into brush, which snapped and rustled with the constant movement of smaller creatures. Not even snakes worried her as much as whatever else she didn't know about.

She moved alongside a stream. Small granite mounds, hung with moss, rose from the banks. Ferns sprouted from more ordinary shrubbery. Weeds and grass swayed rhythmically to the sea breezes, as did the branches of the hissing sycamores. Oak and pine stood proud and sturdy. This forest was so unfamiliar, yet so familiar. In some moments, Zoe found it strange that the Pacific was less than a few miles west of her.

Despite the noise of so many cries and so much movement, an indomitable, entrancing quietness pervaded everything—so much so Zoe began to have second thoughts about hunting anything, for fear of disturbing the forest's peace.

I belong here, too.

She continued streamside, spear half-lowered, half-ready. Around a bend, maybe a hundred yards ahead of her, something violently thrashed the foliage. She stopped, listened to big creature running panicked, issuing guttural, honking noises. More crashing and more footfalls. A final burst of brutality. A strained moan.

Then the beasts, pursuer and prey, fell silent.

For long moments, Zoe stood still.

Her first motion was to move to the other side of the stream, where she continued north, peering further and further around the bend. She tried to step lightly and every twig-snap or crackling leaf heightened her pulse. The amount of blood in her, raucous in flow, felt bigger than she could contain. She was exhilarated.

Walking ahead, she saw a beast bent in furious activity over another. Feasting. Brush covered much of the sight but obstructed none of the grisly sounds: gnawing and splintering and crunching of bone and wet tearing of tissue. Redness stained some of the ferns and foliage. Feasting for sure. The killer's coat was dark tan, its kill an unidentified, hirsute heap, now matted crimson.

The golden death. As if in confirmation, it raised its head. Its two sharp feline eyes, yellow-green like swampy, primordial planets, stared at her.

Zoe was entranced. The massive feline growled, warning against her approach. The cat's head rose, its face revealed in full. Pink rag-tongue curling over its bloodied chops.

The cat lunged. Zoe ran.

The creature lunged from the brush, all tendons taut, sharp ends readied. Zoe didn't even think to raise her spear. In fact she dropped it as she ran, ran and ran, bounding, loping, splashing in mud and gouging her legs on branches and thorns. Constantly in her mind was the possibility of one rock, one stick, one *anything* sending her to the ground, to a gnashing doom.

The cat crashed and bounded. It could easily catch me, she thought. But gradually she got the impression that it sought to drive her away rather than to kill her, because it had its feast—for now.

The land sloped precipitously, but Zoe thought little of it and so burst through the trees and flailed downhill and fell on her side into brush. Her body thundered with ache, particularly her right leg and her face. She twisted down the hill, smashing shrubs, careening off trees, parting whole seas of underbrush creatures.

Finally she came to rest. She breathed. Coughed. Spat. Kept her eyes shut for several bloated, blackened seconds until slowly she opened them and saw, past the trees, and the late sun fingering through them, the large cat at the top of the hill. It peered down at her. Curious? Sympathetic? No. Just ensuring. Warning. Instructing. It stood there, head slightly cocked, watching her intently, its eyes lit with savage superiority—as if it knew her fate better than she.

***

The tribespeople came to her aid and took her promptly to the medicine hut, where, as before, the elderly woman hovered her hands over Zoe and chanted, and she felt again that tingling sensation. The woman held a seashell full of bitter liquid to her lips, and Zoe took two gulps. The room grew blurry, her consciousness loose, tenuous. Smells of pine and tar. She felt outside herself, could watch in ghostly intervals the woman working on relieving her body of its wounds, then wrapping some of them in a wet, leaf-lined cloth.

All throughout, Zoe was detached, unsure if she was dreaming or awake. She assumed she was dreaming when, as if blown by wind, she drifted outside the hut onto the beach, where the village sat oddly quiet and empty, save for a small child who called to her by the fringe of the woods.

He's waiting for me, she thought. She went to the child, feeling heavier, more *there*, the closer she approached. A smile lit the boy's face, and excitedly he led her into the trees.

And with each step, everything around her grew hazy, all textures blurred.

But the world wasn't going away, she realized. Only changing. Life fluids poured into another container, taking shape anew.

Only the faces of the world change, not the forces.

Woodlands stretched into skyscrapers and city buildings, overgrown shrubbery molded into curt, geometric signs like *Coffee* and *Thai Massage* and *24 Hours* and chunky red letters promising *Donuts*.

And Zoe was still walking. She couldn't *not* walk. Her body was suddenly no less than an automaton, traversing a path down a trail now made of concrete. A sidewalk.

The child was still in front of her, but he'd changed, too—grew older, lighter, blonder. The new world was clearing, the creative mists evaporating. The sky seamed with telephone wires and breathy contrails. The air so much heavier and hotter, her every breath hauling an almost physical thing down into her lungs.

"We should walk faster," urged the person in front of her, now a young woman her age. "We shouldn't be late."

The person's face crystallized. Full familiarity returned.

Naomi.

Her friend Naomi was walking eagerly in clip-clopping high heels down the sidewalk.

Traffic choked the street—Melrose Avenue, Zoe noticed by a sign. People bustled in and out of doors and yelled and homeless folks lay unmoving against storefronts.

The energy of the transition nearly overwhelmed Zoe, as if she'd been bathing in water that had suddenly turned viscous and mercurial.

But I'm still walking, she thought, nestling more and more into her old self, her body that had apparently been going mechanically along while she'd been... elsewhere.

"Naomi," Zoe said, stopping. She looked down at herself, attired in a turquoise slip, liberal on leg, a thin, white blouse over her torso. She felt itchy makeup on her face. Her hair tied up. Her feet strapped to cork high heels much like her friend's.

"Zoe, what is it?" Naomi said, arms crossed. "We gotta meet Tye."

"Tye."

"At the sushi place."

Zoe was silent.

"He's my agent, remember? I showed him your pictures. He wants to meet you. That's why you came, right?"

"Naomi," Zoe said, "how did I get here?"

"Huh?" Then, clouds parted in Naomi's expression, a warm empathy brightening. She approached Zoe and gently took her hand. "Come on, no need to freak. I was nervous, too, but Tye's really cool."

"Where's," Zoe started, "where's my car? Did I drive here?"

Naomi eyed her. "Are you okay? I drove us here. Your car's back at my place."

Unsure what to think, Zoe continued on, much as she had before, part of her on a track.

***

Tye Rhodes, scrubbed and smiling, ordered sashimi and roll platters which appeared like succulent rainbows on the table.

Between every chopsticked mouthful, he rattled off glamorous speculation on the young women's careers, how they could be a dynamic duo, "best friends" who together conquer the industry.

"Lots of famous actors were friends," he said. "They helped one another. That's the urban myth about Hollywood, that it's all cutthroat. You'll find a lot of collaboration and cooperation here."

Zoe felt unprepared for Tye's spiel. He said things, observed things, predicted things and all the jargon and enthusiasm made it only into the shallow end of her mind, if that. She had little attention for him. If she were honest with herself, she had little interest, too.

Thinking of the elder by the campfire, how they had so mysteriously yet so clearly spoken in meaning and not vocabulary, she realized whatever mechanism or membrane between them that had made such comprehension possible had hardened into a wall allowing little passage of Tye's words, which were modern and twenty-first century and English but, ultimately, not her language.

To her left, Naomi remained enraptured, and, before it could be debated, leapt instantly at Tye's suggestion of a scenic drive in his BMW through the Hollywood Hills, across Mulholland.

"It'll be a sort of inauguration," Tye said, with a fairy-dusted smile. "Since you're both new here."

"Well, I've been here awhile," Naomi said. "I'm an Angeleno."

"Angelenos are born here, sweetie," Tye said. "Even I'm not an Angeleno."

Tye picked up the check and they left the restaurant. The valet pulled Tye's gleaming vehicle up to the curb and gestured enthusiastically at the open driver's side as Tye slipped him money. Zoe sat in the back while Naomi, brimming with excitement, hunkered in the front. Before Tye got in, she inched her skirt further up her thighs, and straightened her stiff blonde hair.

Get out, said a voice deep within Zoe. *Get out and get away.*

Where had she come from? Increasingly, she could recall very little. Clear memories of her past were whitewashed the closer they got to the present moment, as if everything around her, even her own reactions and movement, had sprung up immaculately, clean and unblemished.. None of this was real. This was a paper-over of the real, of a truth-place where a much more permanent part of her existed. There she could find the *real* her, the her from whose lips she was now a mere exhale.

She was drifting away from some wonderful source.

How did I get here?

Already the car was moving into the Hollywood Hills, through oak-shaded streets connecting lush estates and manors that in their palatial power stood like enduring principles, even though they weren't and could never be. There was a feel here that Zoe didn't like, a forlorn stain on the land, upon which she envisioned phantom currents, sludgy and swollen with wasted dreams and egos— humanity's sewer main, broken and spilled nakedly and odorously about.

They reached Mulholland and wound their way atop the ridge. Tye continued speaking in sparkle-toothed authority. Sprawling views of the San Fernando Valley opened between the trees and houses.

It was wilder up here, Zoe noticed, such wildness bubbling ancient and green below and between everything.

"The valley to the right," said Tye, gesturing, "is of course Hollywood's shadow-cousin, the adult film industry. Funny, it's usually a one-way street, from here to there. No one comes from there to here. Or hardly anyone."

Zoe didn't know how to respond. Neither did Naomi, it seemed.

"But that's not something we'll have to worry about with you girls, right?" Tye said. Quickly he turned to Zoe, his eyes lighted but also savage, superior—as if he knew her fate better than she.

The Encroaching

The first one I saw running across the road, a large shadow skirting my headlights as I drove down Pico Boulevard. I thought it was a cat, albeit an awfully big one. Its size was striking enough for me to slow down and follow it with fixed eyes to the other side of the street, where I saw the busy, striped tail clamber upon the curb.

Three other pairs of gleaming bandit's eyes glared at me as I passed. The sight was so surreal that my brain didn't catch up with my senses until the next red light, and even then it had trouble keeping its footing.

Raccoons? In Santa Monica? The last time I'd seen a raccoon was while camping in Yosemite National Park, and I'd treated it with the same perky little thrill associated with any wildlife encounter.

Yet I soon learned how common these urban ones were, and how increasingly common they'd been the last several years.

"Nick, you never go out at night," teased my neighbor, a six-foot gym teacher named Edwin. "They're all over. Like the possums and rats. You troll the streets often enough you'll see them plenty of places. My brother just got a house in Venice, and his whole front yard was dug up by raccoons."

This wildlife incursion wasn't specific to just raccoons, and, according to my mother, it'd been on the rise for the last half-century.

"I used to never see squirrels around," Mom would say. "But now every time you sit down in your backyard you get some begging little bushy-tail chattering up to you."

The general theory, which I could have deduced without my slight research into the subject, was that the furry visitations resulted from an encroaching humanity that left little choice for the animals but to acclimate to a new steel and concrete wilderness. Survival necessitated them moseying on down from the hills and woods. We were moving into their hoods and, like any good neighbors, they were the first ones to make the greeting. Though what they took and what they left was, indeed, not very welcoming by neighborly standards.

I found articles and message board posts describing some of the diverse wildlife spotted across Los Angeles. A retired police officer talked about seeing a gray fox trotting down the fifth hole of a municipal golf course in West L.A. Coyotes frightened joggers on the gilded roads of Brentwood and Pacific Palisades. Deer grazing by the Getty Museum. Skunks ambling down Century City sidewalks. Even a mountain lion making a midnight visit to the pool area at the Hotel Bel-Air, in the canyonlands behind UCLA.

I've lived in Santa Monica my entire life. I grew up in the south side towards Venice, but in my young adult years have since migrated to the northern borders with Brentwood. I've always sensed something amiss about Los Angeles, and I'm not talking about the infamous gang spots or noir-ish folklore. I'm referring to the more rustic areas, the Santa Monica Mountains, Mulholland Drive, Brentwood Hills, Topanga Canyon—all beautiful, gentrified areas that to me have an eerie vibe, a sensation I've never been able to pinpoint. While other cities stand so permanently and resolutely upon the landscape, this city feels self-conscious and transitory, as though aware of its loitering, aware of its status as a new trespasser in an ancient wilderness which, spring-loaded to return, has only begun to unveil its secrets.

Though that could just be me.

***

The afternoon of Edwin's break-in was gray and damp, a dismal buffer between that morning, which had been clear, and the early autumn night.

Coming home early from the studio, I spied an SMPD cruiser parked outside my house. My chest tightened, as is my natural reaction to police despite my history as a law-abiding citizen, yet no blue-suits stood waiting for me on my front porch. They were next door.

After parking and settling some things inside, I made my way over there just as the officers were leaving, timing it right so I wouldn't have to indulge in any sort of residual questioning.

Edwin's face held an onion-white pallor, and he acted defeated. Looked deflated.

"What happened?" I asked.

"They broke into my house," he said. "I go downtown for a couple hours and I come back and there's a ragged hole in our bedroom window. I swear… in broad daylight, too."

"No one heard or saw anything?"

He shook his head. "The cops asked around. You were at work. So was pretty much everyone else. The nanny over at the Roberts' there thought she heard glass shattering, but that's about it." Ed removed his glasses and rubbed his eyes. "Serves me right for not listening to Dorothy and activating that security system sooner. God, imagine her reaction when she gets home. Think I'll just call her."

A sea breeze picked up and danced over the neighborhood. I shuddered. I wasn't sure whether to console Ed then walk away, or press with more questions.

Before I could make the decision, however, my mouth made it for me.

"What did they take?"

Ed gave me a sour look. "They took what you'd expect those kinds of jerk-offs to take: TV, laptops, Dee's jewelry, all that. I still haven't fully assessed what's missing."

"Well," I said, wanting to kick myself. My gut was aflutter. "Be thankful you weren't here when they came."

"If I was *here* they probably wouldn't have *come*," Ed said. "Damn fine mess. Here I got the house ransacked, and you know what happened last night?" He shook his head. "Those little bugger raccoons came and tore up my backyard, like my brother's. Swear. One scavenger after another."

***

Late that afternoon, I fell asleep on the couch. When I awoke night had already fallen and, for a moment, I felt vulnerable and disoriented. Strangest of all, the dark felt like a thing watching me, creeping closer and closer with morbid curiosity until the light sent it scurrying to the corners like some insectile phantom.

Though my stomach growled, my brain protested louder for nicotine. I sat outside on the balcony, taking sips of smoke under the pale glow of the patio security light disclosing only a quarter of the backyard. I carefully watched the dark end of my property where the trees and shrubs made dark, foreboding silhouettes against the sky, as though the fence ending my yard acted as a border between civilization and untamed wilderness.

My ears perked at a noise above, not far away. I looked up towards the source, which lay beyond the reach of the patio light, and could see movement in one of the trees. Then, as if the night sky itself had come alive, an unexpectedly large, winged creature flew over my head, over the roof, and quickly disappeared. Its white underbelly caught the light, exposing it briefly as an owl.

I blinked, somewhat amazed. I went around to other sections of the house to get a better vantage point on the roof. In all likelihood, though, that feathered grandfather clock of the woods had moved farther on.

***

I've never been good sleeping alone, and the nights following Edwin's break-in found me jumpy, a borderline insomniac by night and, by day, a fervent lock-checker and neurotic surveyor. I stayed mostly indoors.

I tried leaving on some of the lamps while I slept. I stopped this after only two nights, as I found it more difficult to sleep knowing there were lights humming and burning somewhere in the house, regardless of whether I could see them. It was a strange quirk; I couldn't sleep with lights on in the house, and I didn't want to sleep in darkness.

One night, around one, I heard scattered noises downstairs, a kind of clicking and rustling, then the hollow *clop* of a plastic cup being knocked over. I figured whatever might be happening down there was happening in the living room by the coffee table. My dad's gun in hand, I made my way down the creaking stairs, unintentionally announcing my arrival before I was ready to do so.

If the perpetrator was human, he was certainly making little noise, which both elevated and alleviated my fear. If it wasn't human, what was it? And if it was, what in Christ's name allowed him to slink around so very quietly?

Yet not quiet enough, I thought, anger thickening my veins.

I flipped on the light and screamed "Hey!", holding Dad's firearm before me—aimed at none other than a small black rat sitting on the coffee table, chewing potato chip crumbs in furious quivers of its body. It didn't seem to mind my presence.

I laughed, expelling from my imagination all my frightful prior thoughts. I was left with the sobering realization that I now had a rat problem.

Whether the late hour or my relief that it wasn't its human counterpart, I didn't much feel like killing the ravenous rodent. Clearly he didn't sense that danger in me, because he remained still while noshing on the rest of my chips and peering up at me with those pearly black eyes. I felt sorry for him, and thought, in an absurd moment, that he might be seeking shelter from the avenues and alleys now crawling with bigger and better competition.

I quickly dug out the hamster cage I'd had since I was ten. Its first inhabitant had been a hamster named Chester, gifted to me by my late grandmother when I really wanted a dog. Nevertheless, Chester proved a good companion (and distraction buddy) during the protracted study sessions middle school threw at me. I'd ended up keeping his cage, for posterity's sake.

It took longer than hoped to fish out the cage, and I was afraid the rat may have since scurried off to darker corners, but he was still there when I returned, only a foot or two away from his original position on the coffee table. Deciding to try the easy way first, I dropped some scraps in the cage and, very slowly, approached the table, knelt and offered the open enclosure. The rat didn't scamper. He just looked at me curiously.

After some hesitation, he climbed atop the cage. In such proximity I could see the dust on his coat and several scars on his backside. I started to become antsy about being so close to it, wondering if by morning I was still going to want this thing in the house.

Several moments later, he climbed obediently inside and I shut the door. The next day, I named him Cornelius. I decided to keep him. With another body in the house—

however small—I was able to sleep better in the ensuing weeks. Believe it or not.

***

"You'll enjoy this," my mother said over the phone. She always called me on Sundays, usually after returning from her weekly tradition of light hiking in Temescal Canyon with her friend, Bonnie. "Guess what we saw behind the high school."

"What's that?"

"A bobcat," she said. "A bobcat, of all things."

"No kidding," I said, genuinely excited but, after some of my research, not altogether surprised.

"Yep, a bobcat," she said, as though I hadn't heard the first couple times. "But you know, it didn't look like a normal bobcat. Though I'm sure that's what it was."

"Did Bonnie see it, too?"

"She did, yes. She'd never seen one, either. And she's been in the Palisades for almost ten years now."

"What did it look like?"

"That was the funny thing. It didn't have the shaggy, grayish fur. It was sleek and red-orange, with long black ears and really sharp green eyes. And a stubby tail. The stubby tail is what made us decide it was a bobcat. But it looked odd, so when I came home I did research on the internet and you know what?"

"What?"

"The animal it looked most like was something called a Caracal cat. But that's only found in Africa and Asia."

"Hmm."

"Isn't that strange?" I couldn't tell if Mom was more puzzled or excited. "I mean, if that's what it is, what on Earth is it doing here?"

"I have no idea, Mom."

***

There was a noise and my eyes snapped open.

The clock: 2:02 a.m.

I lay there still and tingling, wondering if what I'd just heard had come from my dreams, or downstairs. Either way it was enough to awaken me, to wrench me from a sleep that, while certainly not substantial, was the most I'd gotten in several weeks.

Silence as I waited, listening.

Then a sharp knock—either a dropped object or a clumsy footfall, followed by further noise that was undeniable movement.

There were people in my house. As if to seal this realization, I heard a male voice rasp something under his breath, the only word of which I understood was an obscenity. Chills burst through me.

Moving slowly, I reached for the nightstand and pulled open the drawer and extracted Dad's pistol. From the vicinity of the garbled noises and voices I could tell they were likely coming through the kitchen window, and were having trouble doing so.

That's good, I thought. If they're collected in one spot it'll be easier to drive them out. Pick 'em off, maybe.

If I had the courage to go down there.

I removed the sheets and climbed out of bed. The cold ambushed me and I shivered. Gun in my right hand, I took my cell phone in my left and dialed the police as I made cautious steps towards the door when something stopped everything.

Terrified cries erupted from the intruders. Commotion ensued. Glass shattered. Shouting, panicked voices, now retreating outside. Into the backyard.

The intruders' rapid, unexplained escape increased my confidence, and I charged downstairs with what felt like a manic smile on my face, as though I were somehow responsible for their departure.

"Get the hell *out*!" I screamed. "The police are coming!"

Their voices and footsteps had become the night traffic by the time I was downstairs and assessing the damage. The window above the sink was open and cracked, and two water glasses lay broken on the linoleum. Beyond that, and beyond my own unwashed dishes, there was nothing too out of place. My heart began to slow—though still beating deep and hard—and breath returned to my lungs.

From his cage in the living room, Cornelius squealed. He was perched on his hind legs and pressed against the bars. His little body shivered, perturbed.

Suddenly there was another noise outside, a *thwump*. It sounded like someone had toppled a trash canister. My heart resumed its marathon. My lungs seized up. Cornelius continued his tinny squeaking. I raced to the sliding glass door facing the backyard, now partially lit by the second security light I'd installed since Edwin's break-in.

There I caught sight of an unusually large creature clambering away into the shadows. My assumption of it being the last of the burglars was challenged by my gut, which told me that, while person-shaped, it wasn't a person.

Cautiously I edged out into the yard, where I could see distinct, human-shaped footprints, far too massive for any normal person. The tracks faded the closer they got to the back gate that flapped and creaked wide open. The mild autumn breezes were stained with a rancid, wild odor. I wasn't sure what to make of this, whether these things were all remnants of the burglars, or if I had some other party to thank for scaring them off. Yet that consideration, of course, led to its own brambly maze of disturbing thoughts.

I turned on the backporch light, got my phone and took several close-up shots of the first three footprints, as they appeared the clearest. The flash provided the rest of the illumination for a clear picture, and with several of them in hand I shut off the porch light and headed back inside, trying not to settle too concretely on the identity of the prints—even though they reminded me an awful lot of those that had been sensationally stamped all over screens and pages the last fifty-some-odd years.

This is impossible.

Cornelius kept making noise in his cage. I stopped and looked inside and he stood shuddering and absorbing everything what I imagined to be a kind of anxious glee. He was a rat, the original denizen of the urban crack and crevice, and he looked at me as I looked at him and I imagined he might be thinking something like, *Bigger and better—we ain't alone anymore.*

The Anubis Protocol

1

Ironically, it was when Douglas McGregor knew he was dying that he finally found the weekly card games tolerable. For months, it seemed the conversation around the darkened corners of Abe's Pub had revolved around death and what life might be like afterward. Of course, there was also the debate on whether such as thing as an "afterlife" could indeed be classified as life. Although the rest of the guys had found solace in it—smiling, laughing, wondering, joking—Douglas wasn't sure how to feel. Somewhere between the hollow smile he plastered on his face and the intrinsic fear of physically dying, he was gray, dead air inside.

"I know Cassy's asking questions already," said Vernon Horowitz, yellow teeth clenching a cigar as he tossed new cards into the waiting hands of the group. "She don't tell me, but I know she's checking up on websites already. I saw it on her history cache."

"Eh, they're probably all doing that," said Bernie Johnson. He spread his five cards in front of his eyes, which Douglas saw spark with potential victory.

"I'm out," Douglas said. He threw down his cards. "Hand looks like a foot."

"Does it bother you she's asking questions?" Albert Mason asked Vernon.

"I don't know, should it?"

"It bothers me," Albert said. "That's why I told Robby to not sneak behind my back. When he's ready with the preparations, he'll come to me directly and we'll work through 'em. I don't trust him to design my site after I'm gone."

Douglas stayed quiet as he surveyed his small circle of friends. They'd been coming to the pub every Thursday night for the past fourteen years, once as a large boisterous group of twelve since scythed to about five, usually four now that Frankie was in the home. He wasn't sure whether to tell them or not—none of their friends that had died over the years had ever really said anything beforehand. Their respective stroke, their heart attack, their cancer, whatever did them in was simply the following week's first topic of conversation.

"See, I just as soon stay out of it," Vernon said. "And actually I'm kinda glad Cassy is doing this without my input. I mean, she's the one that's going to have to look at it."

"Has anyone talked to Jud lately? Do you know if his site's up?"

"No idea. I find the whole thing creepy. I remember I once talked with my father and I ended up having bad dreams about it."

"You were a kid though, right?"

There was an embarrassed beat. "No—this was about five years ago."

"Hah! Better get used to it, ol' timer. You wouldn't want Cassy and your granddaughter to get the heebie-jeebies talking to you, would they?"

"Well, that's even if I get approved."

"You'll get approved. You ain't a murderer or a felon or anything, are you?"

"No, but… the war."

"Eh, I wouldn't worry about that. They've changed the software since then. It's not so black 'n white anymore. Besides, the war was a hell of a long time ago now."

"What's the matter, Doug?" Bernie asked.

Having been somehow entranced by the ash tray in the middle of the table, to Doug the surrounding voices had become wordless, meaningless.

"Doug?"

"What?"

"You all right there, sport? You're not dyin' on us, are ya?"

Douglas tried a smile. "Just keep dealing there. I want to get my money back from last week."

"If you want get your money back," Vernon said, "just whip up that card proggie you made."

"I'm surprised you even remember that."

"Oh yeah."

"What was this?"

"Doug here made this card program way back when that would scan the deck and shuffle together these outrageous hands, and it was like mathematically calculated to favor the dealer or something, I can't remember exactly."

"It was a silly little something to pass the time at work,"

Doug said. "When I started at Melnick Labs. Thankfully, I soon got promoted."

"Yeah, and the promotion covered the extra cash you were once makin' with that game."

"I stopped using that program when I got promoted. I got serious."

"Yeah, that's what I mean!"

Conversation dribbled off for a moment. Country music whined from a distant corner.

Doug excused himself from the card table, went to the bar and ordered a scotch on the rocks from Vic the bartender, and it was there he sat, hounded by thought. He had done something, something long ago. He had gotten himself out of it, but it was still there—others had taken over and it had evolved, evolved beyond his wildest dreams. What had happened? *How* had it happened? Talk about the creation slipping from the creator...

No, no, it was stolen from me.

He thought of Helen and Marky, both still so young. A year from now would he still be able to talk with them?

It depended.

2

"My mom showed me how to talk to Grammy last night."

"No, no, you only give me twelve cards," said Marky McGregor, clutching a dozen cards in a broken rickety fan. One of them, a queen of diamonds, fell to the floor. He picked it up.

"I thought it was thirteen."

"No, no. You're wrong…"

"Have any of you talked on the computer?"

"I talk to my grandma all the time on the computer," Ricky Aldridge said. "So I've done it."

"Did she die?"

"Yeah."

Marky fumbled with his oversized hand, the long fan too unwieldy for his childish grip. The cards slid from his grasp.

"I don't think this is the way you're s'posed to play poker," Johnny said.

"Who cares?"

"My grampa taught me how to play," said Larry, the fourth of the bunch.

"So is this right?"

"I dunno."

Four boys sat in the living room of Marky McGregor's home as they pieced together from exaggerated memory their grandfathers' lessons in card games.

"My mom said I might hafta talk to grampa on the computer soon," Marky said. "She said that'll be the only way I get to talk to him."

"I need two sevens," Ricky said. "I only have four."

"You're not supposed to tell other people the cards you need. Geez."

"I think these cards are messed up. I have five nines."

"How do you talk to dead people on the computer?" Marky asked Ricky, who held four cards in his mouth as he redecorated the rest of his hand.

Ricky took the cards out from his mouth. "I dunno how to do it. My mom did it all for me. She just told me when to type."

"And you could talk?" Larry asked.

"Yeah. Some words I couldn't read, but I still got to talk to Grammy."

"Why do people even have to go on the computer?"

"My mom says they grad…grad…gradoo-ated from life."

"Why do they need to leave, though?"

"They don't leave!"

"Then how come we can't see them anymore?"

"I can't talk to my mom because she was bad," Johnny said quietly. "That's what my dad said."

Marky felt aloof from the conversation. He'd never had anyone to speak to on the computer. He'd only been a year old when his father had vanished, and according to Mom his late grandmother, much like Johnny's mother, hadn't made it through the "approval" process, so he couldn't talk to her like his friends could their grandmothers.

The boys continued playing their own version of poker, which soon segued into a variation of gin rummy, then crazy eights, ending up eventually as a pile of discarded cards in the center of the floor. They went on to videogames, which provided Marky with a good distraction from the other room where Grampa and Mom sat. He couldn't hear them, but didn't have a good feeling about whatever they were talking about.

3

Helen McGregor saw a helplessness in her father's face she'd never seen before. The fear, normally contained and kept determinedly at bay, now seemed to have bled through him. His will, his soul, soaked through to transparency. It was made worse by Doug's vain attempt to hide his vulnerability, even though Helen could hear it in his voice, devoid of life and energy. She could see it in his trembling hands and frame. Worse, she could feel it.

"Did Dr. Wright say there was nothing you could do?" Helen asked. "Nothing?"

"It doesn't matter, Helen. The doctor said any procedure would be a fifty-fifty shot, and quite honestly I don't want to spend the remaining months full of tubes and stuck in the hospital going through some awful procedure that will keep me from you and Marky."

Helen nodded, slowly.

Doug sighed. "And, here we go…"

"You know Anubis will read you just fine, right, Dad? You've got nothing to be ashamed of."

There was a pause.

"Dad?"

She took his hand, which was white and clammy, as if death had already begun staking out its territory. Doug looked at her.

"I'm scared, too, but—"

"What do you have to be scared of?" he said. "You don't have to die, you don't have to be packed into some tiny chip… how do I know what it's going to be like?"

"I don't know what it's going to be like, Dad," Helen said, tempering herself. "And don't tell me not to be scared, because I am. I'm scared for you. I'm scared for us and how this might affect your relationship with Marky, our relationship."

"What if I don't even get to talk to you or Marky?"

"Don't say that—"

"What if I'm just floating around… out… *there*." Doug waved a semi-contemptuous hand towards the computer. He made a gesture Helen had seen him make before, one he'd said came from his school days. He would point to his left shoulder, then right, then touch his forehead and lastly his chest as though he were tracing the letter T. Helen had ceased to ask of its significance. Old men and their little habits.

Helen asked, "Do you want anything special on your… your site, Dad? I mean, I know a lot of people design their sites beforehand, but—"

"Doesn't matter to me. Only people that would be really seeing it are you and Marky, right?"

"I suppose… and your pub buddies, don't forget."

"Yeah, if they don't croak before me."

They exchanged weak smiles.

Doug asked, "When are we actually going, by the way?"

"Going…"

"To Anubis, I mean."

"I made an appointment three weeks from now."

"Three weeks?"

"It was the best I could get, Dad, and I think it's best that we know what we're in for with this."

"That's fine, Helen."

They sat quietly for a little while, Doug's harsh breathing and the faraway explosions and yells from Marky's little videogame group filling spaces between every maddening tick of the clock, ticking away toward the transition. Helen held her father's hand, warming its stubborn coldness.

4

The Anubis Headquarters was a stunted tree trunk of a building, almost incomplete in appearance. Looming behind it as some larger, bureaucratic sibling was the county hospital.

They were ushered to the third floor, Orientation & Planning, by a bubbly little round woman whose sheer positivity irritated Helen. She wondered if it was an act, demanded by those who cut her checks, or more the woman's own defensive optimism against the nature of her livelihood. The nature of this place.

They checked in with a short, round man who looked to be the male equivalent of the stocky woman they'd encountered downstairs. Helen had a sudden, outlandish notion that perhaps all of Anubis was run by one family, spawned generations ago in the brain of a man who dreamed of dominating humankind. In lieu of asserting his rule by force, he would wait at the end of their lives, becoming the nod or the wagging finger so desperately sought by everyone in regards to their life lived. The ultimate control.

You're too paranoid.

After check-in they were told to sit and wait for a Ms. Jameson, one of the Personal Family Consultants, a title that struck Helen as redundant. Hung high in the corner of the waiting room was a screen on which looped a video describing Anubis and its history. Doug's sickly eyes were fixed on it. Helen watched him.

"Thank you for visiting Anubis," rang the video's cheery female narrator. "Whatever the nature of your visit, rest assured you or your loved one will be in great hands. Our engineers all over the world have been working hard for many years and many generations to provide the international community with safe and just hereafters. Anubis Network spans the globe, from Asia to the Middle East, all the way up Africa to Europe and over to, of course, our United States, connecting everyone living and dead via the World Wide Web.

"The Anubis Protocol," it continued, "began as a sophisticated polygraph test, to be used in interrogations and trials. The first prototype, at the time dubbed CyberWitness version one, was built a hundred and seventy years ago and has since undergone a significant evolution in both its capabilities and its impact on world culture.

"However, it wasn't until a hundred years ago, when the program came under the hands of Empire Technology, that it emerged as what was then called CyberLife version three, essentially the skeleton program of what we now know…"

The door opened. In poked the amiable face of a young woman, pale skin accentuating the penetrative darkness of her brown eyes.

"Mr. McGregor?" she said.

"Yes?" said Helen.

The woman smiled weakly. "I'm Ms. Jameson. You may follow me."

Jameson stepped in further, holding the door open. Beneath her traditional white lab coat she wore a plaid collared shirt tucked firmly into dark tan slacks.

Doug rose, standing tentatively. Jameson hurried to give Helen a hand in supporting him and, clumped together, the three moved towards the hallway entrance. Doug's breaths were labored, and rippled with phlegm.

Long and stark and empty, the hallway seeped its cold, undeniable history into Helen's blood. She felt like a marcher in some twisted parade, traversing the carpet as she supported her dying father, ushered on by the hazy groping memories of all the dead ones that had made this very same walk.

Jameson's office was at the end of the hallway. When they entered and had eased Doug into a chair, the doctor closed the door and bustled to her desk.

"First, let me just say how sorry I am about the news," said Jameson. "But rest assured, Mr. McGregor, you will live on. The Anubis software has been fashioned to suit innumerable preferences. Assuming your eligibility, of course."

"I'm eligible," Doug breathed. "For what I want."

"May I ask…" Jameson began, then cleared a strand of hair from her face. "May I ask how old you are now, Mr. McGregor?"

"Ninety-four."

"You've lived a good long life."

"I'd like to know more about the nuts and bolts of the process," Helen said. "My mother was... well, she was denied."

"What we do," said Jameson, "plainly put, is scan all the regions of your brain to collect all salvageable data from every aspect of your life. The brain stores everything. Everything you've experienced and how those things have affected your senses, your emotions. Pieces of yourself you might have long forgotten are still there, just buried under mounds of other data, like a messy room. The memories, the consciousness, are transmuted into electrical energy transferred into hardware."

Helen nodded, understanding. Quickly she glanced at Doug—hazy-eyed, he appeared to be daydreaming.

Jameson went on. "What we do is collect all that data, everything down to the first coherent word, and feed it through the Anubis Protocol, which in turn analyzes every bit of information and determines a suitable digital haven for the client. You can expect this process to take about three weeks, sometimes shorter. Rarely beyond that."

Helen cleared her throat and moved to say something, but Douglas beat her to it.

"How does the software separate good from bad?" he said.

Jameson gave a tired smile, clearly too familiar with the inquiry. "The Anubis program has evolved over many years, Mr. McGregor. It knows life isn't simply a matter of good or bad, black or white. The old software used to simply read memories, and it would watch them with a third-party indifference that has since been significantly improved. Now that it collects everything—sensory memory, cell memory, emotion, pain—it reads the whole book instead of just glancing at the cover. Tastes the meal, not the menu.

"What it does…" Jameson clasped her hands together, leaned forward. "What it does to formulate its judgment is read your memories as well as your corresponding emotional history, from which it tailors a suitable afterlife depending on its chemical reading of corticosteroids such as adrenaline and neurotransmitters, anything that might indicate a severely negative reaction to anything you might've done. Privileges, such as the ability to interface directly with the living in our private chat rooms, are afforded to overall good readings. Some privileges may be withheld, depending."

Helen spoke. "Will there be someone to review the final readings?"

Jameson steeled. "No—why would there be?"

"To make sure nothing went wrong."

"Ms. McGregor, I can assure you the Anubis Protocol is failsafe. It's an exceedingly powerful and evolved system, finely tuned over many decades. There is no need to second-guess a machine's scan with a human's. It would only cause delay, and, as you said, room for error."

"So," Helen said, eyes narrowed. "Anubis is more or less… perfect?"

The young doctor leaned back in her chair. "As close as we can get on this Earth, yes."

5

Life left Douglas McGregor at half-past nine on October fifth, two weeks after his ninety-fifth birthday. When it happened the months of logistical and financial preparation held their own while the months of emotional preparation— much as a leaf-pile in a windstorm—fell haphazardly apart.

At his bedside Helen was surrounded by doctors and nurses, including Dr. Wright, her father's primary physician. Vernon Horowitz was also there, sitting across from the hospital bed, head down. Helen left the room, face distorted in tears. She took the elevator down and stumbled out in the courtyard, where she was thankfully alone, and cried.

She thought about calling Marky, but didn't want to interrupt him at school. Perhaps she could call Nadia and have her break the news.

No, that wouldn't be right. You need to tell him.

But Dad would be back. Maybe not in the same form, but he would still have a place in their lives. As a teenager, Marky would chat with him about his first date, getting his license. All the usual milestones.

Dad needs to get through. He needs to be there.

After a slow twenty minutes, she made her way back up towards her father's floor, arms wrapped around herself, cheeks sticky and stained with tears.

When Helen returned, she spied Vernon Horowitz sitting in the hallway, stiff and unmoving as if posing for a portrait.

"Hi, Vern," she said.

Her voice snapped him out of his deadened trance. "Hi, Helen. I'm so sorry. I'm sorry I didn't come to visit him more often. I'm sorry none of us knew…"

"Don't worry about it. I'm sure Dad didn't really want you guys to know."

"Yeah, but dammit… to keep something like this under wraps until suddenly it's just dropped on you like a bowling ball…"

"I know."

"How long did he even know?"

"Not very long. About a few months, I think, before he even told me. I've known for a couple months."

"Guess I should've seen something coming with his dropping out of Abe's every other Thursday or so. I figured he was just getting sick of us old timers and our ways." Vern gave a shallow grin. "Although I'm sure that was part of it, too."

Helen returned the shallow smile.

"They took him up somewhere," Vern said.

"What?"

Vern pointed skyward. "I think he's gone up. Not sure where. I didn't hear it when they were talking. I think they're just getting his body ready." Vern's gaze drifted over Helen. "Here comes the doctor. You can ask him."

Dr. Wright strode towards them, conversing with a nurse who listened intently. When Helen approached them, they abruptly stopped talking, as if out of shame.

"Hello, Ms. McGregor," he said.

"Where's my father? Where did they take him?"

"He's been taken to the Transfer Unit, one floor up. This is standard procedure, no need to worry."

Hesitating, Helen said, "Can I see him?"

Douglas McGregor's body was stretched across a long, metallic table. Three technicians moved about him, one of them adjusting to his head a metal fixture that looked as a cross between a motorcycle helmet and an ancient Roman gladiator helmet. Two knobs jutted from the area covering Douglas' temples and one technician pressed them inward, locking them into place. Draped across the gap between the table and the machinery behind it were three clotheslines of wire connecting the helmet with the computers against the wall, at the center of which stood a large monitor that flickered and buzzed, as if licking its electric chops. Awaiting the feed.

Helen stood there, nurses and doctors passing just behind her.

A painless place, she thought. That's where he'll be. Clean, pure *him*. No sickness, no weakness…

The first decipherable image popped onto the screen, a grainy and spastic memory that seemed to show three children running in a backyard. It was fleeting, synaptic. The monitor went black. Two of the technicians stood over the console, touching buttons and tuning dials, one of them keeping steady watch of her father's body.

Helen realized that the test run had snagged an arbitrary memory. The tears came again. She couldn't watch this. Even if she did, she imagined she'd be able to see very little as they reaped more of her father's ninety-five years. It would flash by too quickly, a snap-cut, hazy movie of so much, so much. Not even the brightest minds could fathom the accumulated mental cargo of a single ordinary person. All were epic tomes. All were walking libraries, breathing universes.

6

With each day she exercised yet more restraint in not phoning the headquarters. The hours offered their distractions—work, taking Marky to school, helping him with homework—but underscoring all of it was prickly anxiousness, now growing into a rash on her mind. It'd been a week.

Only a week.

After two weeks, Helen called. They told her nothing. Nothing to report. Douglas McGregor—or, Patient H55567437899-#BP00—was still undergoing scrutiny.

Marky asked when he would get to talk to grandpa.

"Soon, sweetie," Helen said. "I just have to hear back from the people that are judging grandpa."

"I thought it was a machine that judged grampa."

"Well, it's a machine made by people. And it will be people that tell us when grandpa is back."

***

.then the world turned on, and like a sputtering engine it coughed and blinked and woke up, righted itself, all of its gears and pistons sliding into place as the explosive sensory renaissance met him there in the void.

It was coming, Douglas knew, and it was right.

7

No.

She read the letter again, her fourth time in five minutes.

Helen went to the phone and called the headquarters. They put her on hold and after ten minutes of dead air she hung up then paced the kitchen, head down, thoughts aflurry. What had happened? Why had this happened?

She tried calling again, this time leaving a voicemail for Ms. Jameson. She also tried calling the hospital's Transfer Unit but after another hold, this time of fifteen minutes, Helen took a long breath and then sat down, staring and shivering.

***

Clearly Mom was upset because of something to do with Grampa. But why? Wasn't he coming back on the computer? That was how Marky understood it. Sure it was sad he wasn't going to be around really anymore, but he'd still be there. Kind of.

Something, however, was wrong.

"There's a delay in getting Grandpa online," was what Mom told him one evening at the kitchen table. She was so distant and cold.

Marky chewed on a fish stick. "What's a dul-lay?"

"Means we won't know for a while," she said.

Helen got up and kissed Marky on the head. The kiss felt more obligatory than loving.

"Did you finish all your homework?" she asked. "Because

it's almost bedtime. I'm sorry about the late dinner, too, sweetie, I just… I just have too many things to do."

"It's okay, Mom."

"So did you do all your homework with Nadia?"

"I just had reading to do, that was all," he said. "And I had to finish the handwriting packet."

"All right."

"Mom…"

"Yes?"

"Ricky asked if I could sleep over tomorrow night. Can I go? Please?"

"That's fine. I can take you over there after school."

"Ricky said to come around five, because they have to get his brother at the airport."

"What's the brother's name again?"

"Leonard."

"Oh, right." Mom thought for a moment. "I'll take you at five then. And I'll come get you around noon on Saturday, okay?"

"Okay."

"With no fussing, or whining, or any 'But Moms,' got it?"

"But Mom…"

Marky smiled, shoving the last of the fish stick through his lips. His mom smiled, brighter than she had recently, then leaned in once more and kissed his shaggy scalp.

***

The Alridge household was different that evening. In her movements Ricky's mom Diana didn't so much move as spasm. Ricky's dad, Steven, was also much quieter than usual, preferring to sink into the television or newspaper, offering only courtesy interaction with Marky and even Ricky.

Was it Leonard? That seemed the only major difference now, him being home. According to Ricky he'd been at college and was now visiting. But, save for the bags by the door, there was little evidence of a fourth body in the household.

"Where's Leonard?" Marky asked as they played videogames in Ricky's room.

"He spends a lot of time in the basement," Ricky said. "When he's home, I mean. It makes my parents kinda mad, but they stopped arguing about it a long time ago."

"Why does he go to the basement?"

Ricky shrugged, his thumbs bouncing frenetically about the controller. "I dunno. I looked down there one time and there was a computer and printer and stuff down there." Ricky had much of his concentration on the videogame in front of them. "I think he probably just plays games down there. Games Mom doesn't like."

"Weird." Now that they were on the subject, Marky's curiosity overrode his instinct to be polite. "That's why your mom and dad are mad?"

"Mom and Dad are always mad when Leo comes home. I hate it. And it feels like it's getting worse."

Marky remained quiet. They played for a little while longer, until Diana tapped quietly on the door and informed them, in a low, tired voice, that dinner was ready.

***

Both Ricky and Marky were halfway through their piles of spaghetti when Leonard finally appeared at the table, sliding into a seat next to his mother. A robot on autopilot, was Marky's first thought. He was a thin guy, dressed in oversized clothes as if attempting vainly to add fabric where there was no muscle. His hair was wild, each strand a feral stranger to a comb, and his glasses looked like sawed-off bottoms of soda bottles.

"So I guess I just serve myself," Leonard said.

Steven Aldridge nodded, chewing.

"So how has this semester been, Leo?" Diana asked. "We won't get any surprises this year, I hope?"

"No. Everything's fine. I go to all my classes." Leonard began piling spaghetti on his plate. Marky watched with quiet awe how much went on there. How was Leonard so thin?

"What about the whole living situation?" Steven asked. "Still roommates with that Carl?"

"No, Dad, I'm not. I moved out of the dorms. I'm a sophomore, so I've moved into an on-campus apartment."

"With Carl?"

"No. Carl dropped out. Didn't I tell you that?"

"I don't think so, but it certainly doesn't surprise me. That guy smelled like…"

"Okay I think we've had enough of that," Diana said, motioning with her eyes towards the two children. Then she turned to Marky. "How are you and your mom holding up, Marky? I was so sorry to hear about your grandfather."

"She's doing okay, kinda," Marky said.

"Have they put him online yet?" Diana asked. "I

remember when my mother died. It was hard waiting through the judgment process, but such a relief when I got the word that she was up and available."

Unsaid thoughts haunted the air. Marky shifted in his seat.

"Now we talk almost every night," Diana said. She threw a burning glance at Leonard.

"My mom's mad cuz Grampa isn't on yet," Marky said. "She thinks something's wrong."

"Of course something's wrong," Leonard burst in. He was dousing his spaghetti in parmesan cheese. With his other hand he kept his glasses from sliding off his nose.

"Leonard, please," said Diana. "Not now."

"This kind of thing happens all over the world with Anubis," Leonard continued. "Your mom is one of many, Marky. One of many."

"Leonard—"

"You've switched majors, right Leonard?" said Steven, another attempt to change the subject. "You're doing computer science now?"

"Yeah."

Marky felt an elbow nudge his arm. It was Ricky.

"By the way," he said. "I learned a new card game from Kevin. We can play it after dinner."

"Cool," Marky said. "I think I'm done actually."

"Me too." Ricky put down his fork. "Can we be excused, please?"

***

"So we just keep turning over cards, and whoever gets a higher card each time gets to grab all the cards." Ricky fumbled as he tried to shuffle the deck, doing it more for practice than to randomize the cards. "It's called 'War.'"

"So we just pick out the top card?" Marky said.

"Yup."

"But we won't know what it is, will we?"

"Duh, of course not. That's what makes the game fun. It's all up in the air."

"Okay. That's cool."

Enclosed once more in Ricky's room, the two boys spent the next half-hour in playing card warfare, their lips constantly moistened, their fingers constantly twitchy in the anticipation of overturning the next card, their mouths armed both with groans of defeat and shouts of triumph depending on what came up.

Around nine o'clock Diana tapped on the door.

"Boys? It's time for bed."

"Okay, Mom."

"Oh, and Ricky." Diana opened the door, popped her head in. "Come to the computer, because Grammy wants to say goodnight."

Marky glanced at the clock. Almost midnight.

He had to pee.

Careful not to wake Ricky, who stirred in his sleep more than anyone Marky knew, he crawled from his sleeping bag and tiptoed toward the door. He made his way out to the end of the hallway, feeling utterly naked in the silent house.

When he finished in the bathroom, Marky's heart was jolted by the sudden presence of Leonard, waiting for him as he came out.

"Hey," said Leonard, his face much more alive than it had been earlier in the evening.

"Hi," Marky said.

"Hey hold on for a bit," he said, and went into the bathroom himself. Marky stood cold in the corridor, shivers increasing.

The toilet flushed and Leonard returned.

"Hey kid, you got a sec?"

"What?"

"A sec, a second. Come down to the basement real quick."

"Um…"

Marky glanced back towards Ricky's room, as if seeking approval from the sleep-dead darkness.

"It'll only be a minute," Leonard said.

Feeling oddly privileged, Marky followed him carefully down the basement stairs, their path lit by the pulsing blue glow of a computer screen.

"Check it out," Leonard said. He sat at his computer, whose screen displayed a website with the word SATAN imprinted in bold crimson across the top. Marky couldn't read much else on the page, only scattered words, and it took him several seconds for his stunted reading skills to piece together a proper pronunciation. When he did, there was an inquisitive rise in his voice.

"I belong to this group," Leonard said. "Stands for the Systematic Annihilation of The Anubis Network, but it works because it forms the acronym of evil, and that's what Anubis is—evil. Do you know what Satan is? Or used to be?"

Marky shook his head.

"Hardly anyone does. Hardly anyone knows or believes anything now."

Marky felt vulnerable, partly because of Leonard, mostly because of the pitch-black shadows beyond the reach of the glowing monitor.

"The whole Anubis thing is bullshit," said Leonard. "They've turned dying into something like school graduation, and they claim to be failsafe, but trust me, any machine, any software, is by no means perfect.

"The whole thing doesn't put anyone else at ease, either. It makes it worse. I know this is kind of a bad thing to say, but in some ways I hope your grandfather doesn't get uploaded, because it'll give you and your mom peace. There won't be that ache of having him there but not. Not being able to see him or touch or feel him. It's a half-baked existence."

Marky shifted his weight from one foot to the other.

"I just wanted you to see this, Marky, because you're young and part of a new generation. Understand that there's more to the cycle of life, and the Anubis Corporation has taken it away. There has to be more, but when we die we are just funneled into their hands. It's because everyone is too fucking afraid. Well I'm afraid of them. You should be too. Did you know its primary method of judgment is based off your own emotional record? That means that if some serial killer felt good about butchering eighty children then Anubis would read that as a positive trait. And it's unfair, too. Not everyone is uploaded. It's mostly the ones who die slow and naturally, those who would theoretically have time to say goodbye. But someone who dies decapitated in a car crash – what can Anubis do for them? Nothing."

Marky stood blank and shivering. "Can I go back upstairs?"

"One sec," Leonard said. "I know you probably don't get a lot of what I'm saying, but that's okay. Just want to expose you early on. And I wanted to tell somebody. This whole Satan thing is secret—I mean, I haven't even met the other members in person, but we're all over the world."

Marky thought of Grampa. "So are you breaking Anubis? My Grampa—"

"That's the hope. We started off as a petition, but we turned into a movement. We're working on making it sick. Hopefully halting it for a long time so people can keep living their lives, move on, so widows and widowers can find new spouses without shutting down with guilt and grief." Leonard sighed. "Sorry. You can go."

Marky nodded. Upon reaching the stairs he turned and said, "I won't tell anyone."

Leonard smiled wanly. "Thanks."

He climbed the stairs. When he was back in the cool hallway he realized he needed to go to the bathroom again. On his way there, and during his twenty seconds by the toilet, he thought of what Leonard had said. Was he why Mom was upset? Was it that Satan thing? Were they doing something to prevent Grampa from going up on the computer?

But you promised not to say anything.

His mind kept going until it hit the pillow, where it began its slow wind-down, easing its revolution, creaking to a restful stop.

8

Helen McGregor surprised herself by making a thunderous entrance to the third-floor suite of Halbrook & Lenon, legal offices recommended by Diana Aldridge.

"I want an explanation from the Anubis people," Helen said to the young lawyer, an African-American man named Stewart Jones. "I want to know what's happened to my father, and no one seems to know anything, or no one is telling me anything."

"Ms. McGregor, just calm down."

"I mean, honestly, this must happen a lot, right? Why can't there be a more… you know, solid way of handling it? It's driving me crazy. I guess that's why I came here."

"First of all, Ms. McGregor, I'm not even sure what you're referring to."

Helen threw the notice onto the desk. Jones picked it up and looked at it.

To Whom it May Concern:

It is our regret that Patient II55567437899-#BP00, Douglas Henry McGregor, was scanned

and judged ineligible of full Anubis Protocol privileges. He will be stored and subsequently supplied the appropriate consequences. We apologize for any inconvenience.

"That's what I'm referring to," she said. "They send this to me and they give me no reason or explanation, or any way of finding out what's gone wrong."

"Are you sure your father's reading would've been positive?"

"What are you saying?"

"I'm not really saying anything. But it's not unheard of for people to live several lives before they settle into one they're comfortable with, or one they're willing to share with others. Anubis simply weighs it all."

"But I know my father. He's a good man. There's no way I can get some answer?"

"You've tried calling, I assume? And going to see them in pers—"

"Yes yes, I've tried every which way, but they brush me off like I'm some mosquito in their ear." Helen crossed her arms. She breathed hard. "Have you ever heard of a group called Satan?"

Jones sat back. "I'm familiar with them. Why?"

"My son told me something about them recently. He said they hate Anubis and want to destroy it. Is it possible they could have done something to screw up the system?"

"No, I highly doubt that—"

"Why? How do you know?"

"Because the Satan group is nothing more than a group of whiny, college-aged cyber-terrorists. It was formed by a disgruntled engineer who quit Anubis, if I recall correctly, and he's since been apprehended. They paint themselves as much more of a threat than they are."

Helen paced back and forth.

"You should know, too, Ms. McGregor," said Jones. "That about forty years ago a law was passed protecting Anubis from legal action should an unexpected reading occur that prevented the deceased from attaining full afterlife privileges. Of course, there weren't many lawsuits to begin with, because everyone was a little afraid of attacking the place that would see them into the afterlife. So basically, if you're looking to sue…"

"I'm not looking to sue anyone. I just want to know what happened in my father's reading. I mean, look at the letter—they had plenty of space to write a simple paragraph explaining what they found."

"Would you want to know what they found?"

Helen stopped.

"Listen," Jones said. "The same law that gave Anubis that legal shield also stated that discourse with the creator of the software should be publicly accessible so long as you have court-appointed permission to do so."

"Do you think they'd allow me to speak with him, or her?"

"Him, I believe. He acts as the main server of the network and could very possibly pull up the information you're looking for. The only choice you have to make is this: would you want to drop this now and preserve the memory of your father as is, or do you want to risk discovering something about him that could scar such a memory?"

"My father was just human," Helen said, sitting on the edge of a chair. "I'd like to try and get that court order."

9

"You have thirty minutes," said the woman as she led Helen into a small office. Long tables were aligned against the walls, and stacked atop the tables, like an array of duplicate shooting-game targets, were computer monitors. Many of the computers were vacant—only six were occupied by other people.

"Thank you," Helen said, and the woman left the room. Helen chose a monitor that seemed furthest from any of the others, slung her purse over the chair, and settled in.

The computer sensed her presence and sprung to life, telling her to wait as it ran through several rudimentary start-up tests. She readied her fingers over the keyboard.

Finally it acknowledged her.

Anubis670-9: Hello, Ms. Helen McGregor.

Helen: Hello

Anubis670-9: Before we begin, can I ask you to input the number of the patient?

Helen: H55567437899-#BP00

A load bar scrolled fast across the screen.

Anubis670-9: Thank you, Ms. McGregor. Or can I call you Helen?

Helen: That's fine, I guess.

Anubis670-9: Now I'm assuming you are here because you are concerned about a Douglas H. McGregor?

Helen: Yes I am.

Anubis670-9: He was your father, I presume?

Helen: Yes, of course.

Anubis670-9: Do you believe he was misjudged?

Helen: Yes, he was. You probably think I'm the one making the mistake, that I didn't know something about my father when he was alive...

Anubis670-9: Everyone believes they know more than they do. The Protocol never makes mistakes.

Helen: Yes, okay, but I really just want to know what is going on, PLEASE can you tell me. My father was a good man, and if I can't talk to him any more I would at least like to know why.

Anubis670-9: Let me run the scan for you.

Helen: Thank you

Helen's fingers remained poised over the keyboard, shading it from the harsh blaze of the fluorescent light buzzing above. When the online presence didn't answer for two minutes she began to get severely anxious.

One of the other six people in the room, a woman, began crying, face buried in her hands.

Helen: Hello? Where'd you go?

Anubis670-9: The software respects the wishes of the dead. If there are secrets left untold to members of the family, we do not and will not divulge them once they are deceased.

<u>Helen:</u> Please just let me know what you found.

<u>Anubis670-9:</u> Douglas McGregor is currently in an unclassified state. The consequence of his punishment(s) is largely based on his own self-infliction.

<u>Helen:</u> Are you saying he WANTS to be cut off from us?

<u>Anubis670-9:</u> The judgment of one lies largely in the judgment imparted by the one's self. Douglas McGregor simply does not meet the requirements for full afterlife privileges.

<u>Helen:</u> But WHY? WHAT FOR?

<u>Anubis670-9:</u> I truly apologize, Ms. McGregor, but that information cannot be divulged.

<u>Helen:</u> PLEASE

Promptly the computer shut off. Helen shuddered, sat staring at the starless, black cosmos of the screen until the service woman entered and tapped her shoulder and said it was time to go.

Exhausted and drained, Helen put up no argument.

10

Within a week, Helen sold the computer. She rarely used it anymore and figured maybe she could buy Marky one for school, one they could set up in his room. Away from her.

Several days later, Vernon Horowitz came by, holding a cardboard box.

"I thought you might be interested in some of these," he said. "A lot of it was your Dad's. Well, all of it is, now that I've taken the other stuff out."

Helen opened the door and ushered him in. Vernon

seemed to have aged considerably since she last saw him at the hospital. His face was crinkled and lumpy, his eyes sunken.

He shuffled his way through the door, relaying the box to Helen. "How are you? How have you been?"

"Been okay," Helen said.

"Right."

"I sold our computer."

"Oh?"

"Yeah. Couldn't really stand to look at it with all that happened."

"Where's Marky?"

"He's in school."

"Oh, of course."

The two of them stood in the entryway, Vern with his hands in his pockets, slightly hunched, Helen holding the container.

"Anyway, I thought I'd just bring that by, and… uh… yeah." Vern brought his hands out of his pockets and folded them over one another. Then he turned, regarded Helen. "The boys and I miss him, down at Abe's. We've lost a lotta guys in recent years, but Doug hit us hard. Hit me hard, that's for sure. Been a long time. I'm just sorry we won't be able to talk to him anymore."

Setting the container down on the dining room table and trying to fight back tears, Helen asked, "Where did this stuff come from? You've had it all this time?"

"These're just things from when we worked at Melnick," he said. "I borrowed a lot of his stuff, including his time. He was kind of my mentor, even when I was his supervisor." Vern chuckled. It turned to coughing, through which he defiantly continued laughing. "We stuck together even though we eventually got split up on different projects. He got assigned to some big, secret thing. In fact, that's probably why he became so private—his job trained him, or that project did." Vern rubbed his eyes. "I just ended up with a lot of things from that time. Haven't set eyes on them in decades. Surprised I still have some of them, actually."

The box was packed with old-time books, books on computer engineering, golf, or aviation, one of her father's old hobbies before she had been born. As Helen dug, their accumulated dust fumed up around her.

At the bottom was a small black book, thoroughly bullied by the years, its covers and pages frayed and peeling. It was extremely old, and Helen could barely make out the two words imprinted in modest pride across the cover.

HOLY BIBLE

It sounded familiar to her, but she couldn't place it. She opened it and out fell a disc that struck the corner of the table and landed flat on the floor.

"What is this?"

"Not sure," Vern said. "With my eyes I can't tell anything anymore."

Helen picked it up. On the disc was a simple label in bold print. When she looked at it, she had to look again, assuming instinctively that it had to be wrong, or some kind of prank.

CyberLife

v 3.0

Douglas McGregor

Senior Engineer

Melnick Labs

A division of Empire Technology

High Stakes

If Thursday night had been any busier, Joe Mullard probably wouldn't have noticed the two guys who took the corner pool table. They were professionals, tried and true, their suits groomed and pressed with an ironing of success. What Joe didn't understand was what the hell they were doing walking into Castle Bar in the first place.

"Can I get you guys anything?"

His voice cut the ribbon of their conversation. They looked back at Joe, smiling almost patronizingly.

"Do I want anything?" one of the men replied. "I'm not sure. This place always brings the alcoholic out in me."

"You're not kidding," said his friend.

"The last time I was drunk here I had a kid," the first man said. "She was married, too. I got the hell out of there for a while."

"Well. I wouldn't say that necessarily."

"True, you certainly had a field day with that one."

Suppressing a frown, Joe said, "Sure you guys don't want anything?"

"No, thank you, we're fine."

"Okay, boys."

One of the men went to claim the corner table. The other began to follow, then hesitated. He leaned over, casually resting his elbow on the counter like a sleazy executive about to rub his fingers together in a gesture of *I can make it worth your while*.

"Mr. Mullard."

Joe's ears perked up. At the moment, the fact that this well-kempt businessman knew his name wasn't weird. It kind of made sense—in a quirky sort of way.

"You can put your worries to rest about your niece," he assured Joe. "I've been polishing my billiards ability."

"Excuse me?"

The man knocked on the wooden counter, as though for good luck, then went off to the corner to join his friend, now shuffling the billiard balls into breaking position.

How'd he know me? About Jasmine? Joe wondered. Maybe a friend of hers, he figured, or an acquaintance close enough to know of her vehicle's crippling brush with a drunk-driving Harold Robeson, a regular at Castle whose intoxication Joe had been ironically responsible for that night.

"Ready for a beat down?" the second man said with playful malice.

"Name the stakes, bitch boy."

Joe kept one ear on them as they smothered the tips of their cues with chalk. Frat boy rivalry came out of their mouths, yet the tone was flat, businesslike, a bizarre combination.

"Okay, we'll play the pockets then," said the first man. "Three pockets for Salvation, three for Damnation."

"Good, the classic. You want to break?"

Castle Bar was getting busier, filling with the usual two kinds of people. Young bar hoppers came in and out while the regulars, the guy-guys, their stomachs all looking as though they'd swallowed three volleyballs, nestled in for a night of what usually began in glass-touching merriment but ended in staggering and tears.

There was a harsh smack-clatter of billiard balls. The first man had broken.

"Nothing in," his friend teased. "Now watch how it's done."

The second man took aim and pounded the nine ball into the far corner pocket. He stood back, broadcasting his pride with a loud and bright smile. The first man pinched the bridge of his nose, as if a headache dawned.

"Worlds or Souls?" he sighed.

"Hmm, I'm feeling personal. Let's play Souls."

Castle Bar swelled at an unusual pace for a Thursday. Bobby had started his shift already, taking some of the load off Joe's shoulders. A valley of people surrounded him now. They painted the air with alcohol breath, temporarily forgetting there was a world beyond the pint. Joe had a strange feeling that he was at the center of everything, that this dingy little San Francisco bar was the bullseye in some perfect cosmic circle.

He felt steady eyes on him all of a sudden, and knew without a doubt where they came from. Joe peered towards the two suits, both of whom orbited a chaotic solar system of balls in green-velvet space. One man squinted, analyzing

123

a possible shot as he chalked his cue tip.

The first man, however, the one who had spoken to Joe about his niece, looked towards him and winked. He assumed the position, determined, sharply eyeing the ball at the end of the cue. His tongue poked its way into the musty light, flattened against his upper lip in solemn concentration.

"The soul of Jasmine Mullard," he said. "In the corner Salvation pocket."

One sharp jab later, the cue ball glanced off the striped ten ball, sending it into a rapid sunset below the rim of the pocket.

"Nothin' but net," the man beamed. "Eat that."

The second man smirked, shook his head. "Albert Gershwin, middle Damnation pocket."

The phone rang twice before Joe heard it. He finished pouring a vodka cranberry for a lovely petite blonde, who gave him a thin, disinterested smile. He returned the smile until the phone reached his ear.

"Joe?" blubbered the voice on the other end.

"Mom?" His gut stirred. Seldom did she call him at work, usually complaining she could never hear him over the rugged purr of the bar crowds. "What's wrong? What is it?"

"It's Jazzy," Denise Mullard said. "She just slipped away from us. I... I don't understand, she was doing so much better..."

Oh God. Joe's chest ablaze. Burning.

From the darkened pool table, the first man glanced in his direction, an apology on his face.

Oh God Oh God Oh God No what have I done?

"…I was holding her hand at the time…" his mother cried.

Joe slipped the receiver back into its cradle and stared blankly at someone's quarter-empty beer glass.

"Bobby?" he tried to say with the least emotional crack in his voice.

"Yeah, Joe?"

"I'm gonna, um, step outside for a smoke. I'll be right back."

Bobby, in the midst of pouring water for a woman, nodded his head and gave a thumbs-up with his free hand. Joe was envious of the boy, who had just popped out of bartending school and had so much before him. Castle was just a pit stop for him. Yet Joe also knew that life wouldn't ignore Bobby, as it never let anyone off the hook—youth was just wet cement, awaiting the inevitable vandals.

Outside the air was cold and salty. He lit a cigarette.

Jasmine is dead.

Within a good five minutes the cancer stick ate itself, and by the time it met the ground and subsequently the bottom of his shoe, Joe Mullard felt emptier than ever.

Jasmine, the closest you've ever come to a daughter, is dead. And she won't be coming back. You know why, Mr. Mullard?

He headed back towards the door, holding it open for two ladies sure to leave after getting an eyeful of the tavern's interior. He followed them in.

Another billiard ball smack.

The suits' pool game was almost finished. In the middle of the table lay the solitary eight ball, a wayward eye throwing a sightless gaze at the ceiling. The two men stood holding their cues with imperial authority, like staff-toting palace guards.

"Your shot," said the first man, adding with jest, "No pressure."

Joe's chest began twisting into a hot, breathless knot. He kept seeing Jasmine. Jasmine as a grade-schooler, eagerly trying to tag along with him and his buddies. Jasmine as a strikingly beautiful teenager. Jasmine stuck between tears and joyful shouts as she packed for her freshman year at Colorado State. He couldn't believe she was gone, and it was all because of him, all because of him, the morbid irony of letting Harry-fucking-Robeson feign sobriety and get away with it, letting his inebriated hands grasp a wheel and steer Jasmine Mullard's life into a rapid and miserable twilight.

A large gag of disgust, of self-loathing, coalesced in his throat. Joe began feeling for something in the space of the cupboards below. His hands hopped like eager frogs over Lost & Found bins, recycle boxes and other miscellaneous crap, until finally landing on the desired object tucked far back behind three empty Jack Daniels bottles.

There was another clattering *smack* of billiard balls, this time from the other table. Several guys had started up a game.

Joe cautiously retrieved the gun—which was wrapped in a tattered green towel—and carried it like a dirty diaper towards the bathroom. Once inside, he waited until one of the pot-bellied regulars had finished at the urinal before unraveling the towel.

Out on the tavern floor, the second man said, "This one's for our gracious bartender."

He leaned down and readied his eight ball shot.

"Damnation, corner pocket."

1111

It was all over the news: the McCarran baby had been found, safe and unharmed, in a dumpy trailer owned by Allison Wilcox, a thirty-five-year-old waitress living three states away from the McCarran family. Missing for several weeks, the prospect of finding the baby—an infant boy named Joseph—had appeared hopeless, and the investigation had turned federal when evidence had surfaced that Joseph's kidnapper had crossed state lines.

Agent David Aaronson was by his wife's side at Morris County Hospital when he received the call, and the news brightened him. It brightened Susan, as well, as she knew how much the case had meant to him. Yet through all the headaches and late hours, David had kept his wife at the fore, knowing time was running thin and that, despite doctors' hopeful projections, the cancer would be inevitably victorious.

"This is truly a miracle," stated a teary-eyed Ellen McCarran, Joseph's mother, at a televised press conference. Her husband John had a firm arm around her shoulder. "It's proof that prayers are answered. It's proof that, if you never give up, if you keep hope alive, your prayers will come true."

Susan smiled weakly at the television. She was due for

surgery in two hours, and although he wanted to stay until she was wheeled in, David was also anxious to partake in the interrogation of Wilcox.

His cell phone rang. It was his partner Richard Latham. He took the call and fired quick, appeasing answers at Latham. Then he turned and squeezed Susan's hand.

"Will you be here when I wake up?" she asked.

"I can't guarantee that," said Aaronson, fighting back tears. "But of course I'll try my best."

***

Allison Wilcox looked like she'd just stepped off a twenty-hour flight. She was baggy-eyed, frizzy-haired, worn out. One thing she wasn't: nervous. The agents encircling her, Aaronson included, may as well have been invisible. Her eyes were concrete. She sat still and slumped and, as they spoke, made no indication that she could hear them or was paying any sort of attention. Initial questioning brought wasted energy—she responded mostly in neutral *yeses* or *noes*.

Then, after a half-hour of this dance, her lips, to Aaronson's surprise, moved beyond one syllable.

"If your car was stolen, Agent Aaronson," said Wilcox. "You'd want it back, wouldn't you?"

"Yes…"

"Well, what if the thief gave it to someone else? Does that make it suddenly theirs, negating your ownership?"

He and Latham were silent.

"That baby, Joseph whatever, is mine. He was taken from me, and given to those people. I had so many things I wanted to do, to experience with Ryan, and now it's them that get to… get to…"

Aaronson held up a hand. "Hold the phone. Ryan? Who's Ryan?"

"My son. Or, I guess, was my son. The anniversary of his death is in three months."

"Your son is dead."

"Yes."

"I'm sorry, Ms. Wilcox."

"No you're not. And you don't have to be, because his body died. He didn't. He's been recycled as Joseph, and he still belongs to me."

"So Ryan was…" He waved his hand, inviting her to finish. She didn't.

Wilcox nodded.

"So how do you know your son was… reincarnated as Joseph McCarran?"

"The Follower told me."

"Follower."

"Yes. His services aren't made public, of course—hardly anyone would believe in such a thing. But he is for real, and he tracks people's return. Where they go. Where they end up. He told me Ryan had been moved to Joseph."

Aaronson and Latham shared a glance.

"And you just took it at this person's word that a stranger's baby was really your son?" Aaronson asked.

Wilcox nodded. "Usually a child's memory of their past life burns the brightest when they're infants, but by the time they get to be three the memories begin to fade. That's why

I had to get to him before anyone else, before the new life as Joseph totally destroyed any hope of him remembering his life with me, his *true* life."

"I see," Latham said. "So this Follower… how did you contact him? Meet up at Starbucks?"

"Of course not. I've never seen his face. I don't think anyone has, or can. You call him."

"Call him."

"Yes."

"What's the number?"

Wilcox steeled, her first truly emotional reaction. She looked at Latham, then at him.

"You dial 1-1-1-1."

"That's four ones, you said?"

She nodded, slowly.

"Well, why don't I give him a call right now?" Aaronson challenged, fishing out his phone.

The woman gave him a steady, burning look. Knowledge haunted her eyes. He couldn't tell if she was more burdened or empowered by what she knew, or what she thought she knew.

"You can't call him now," she said.

He stopped, phone open and thumb poised to dial. "Oh? Why not?"

"Do you have anyone to follow?"

"Do I have anyone to follow?"

"Yes, is there any soul you want to follow?" She grew visibly impatient, which offended him.

Aaronson said, "No, no soul."

"Then you won't be able to reach him."

The whole interrogation was beginning to smell bad.

"So this guy's like Santa Claus?" Latham quipped. "Knows when you're awake?"

"Look, don't patronize me…"

Aaronson turned his back to Wilcox and Latham, dialed 1-1-1-1 and pressed *Send*. In soft drones the interrogation continued behind him. There was dead calm as the signals reached out blindly for connection. Dead air. Then the familiar chime of a misdialed number.

***

"How did it go?" Susan asked.

"It went fine," Aaronson said, giving her cold hand a plump squeeze. "The woman is crazy. She was just… I don't know… It's hard for me to even describe it. She was just gone. She wasn't there. Frankly I'm not sure she was in her right mind when she took that baby."

"She thought it was hers, right?"

"Something like that." Aaronson wanted to recount the interrogation and Wilcox's claims, but held back. Susan teetered on the edge of consciousness, and at best heard his every other word.

"People do crazy things," she said. "Love, you know. If that woman thought she was really the baby's mother…"

Her words trailed off. Her chest heaved. He told her not to worry about it, that he understood everything she said.

For the next few days David Aaronson made a second home out of Susan's hospital room. He stayed with her through the late hours, and during work tried to busy his mind with enough tasks to hold off thoughts of his next visit, to distract his imagination from making the phone ring with the dreaded call, or from seeing her face, drained of will as the treatments did nothing but marginally extend her life.

And on November fourteenth at 10:52 pm, Aaronson was with her, and knew it when it happened.

Susan receded into herself, sliding further back, away and away, until life no longer shone on her face. A gray that wasn't cold or warm took its place, hardening her skin, drying and soaking up the last drops of Susan Aaronson.

He was still squeezing her hand, which had since become stiff, as he sat and tried to accept, to know, to make sense of it all, and then he shuddered and began to cry.

***

He was spared the quiet torment of a funeral. Susan Aaronson's body had been willed to the medical department of Johns Hopkins University, leaving no tombstone and no physical presence to scratch at his mind. He had been let go.

Eventually her body was cremated and Aaronson was given the ashes. He scattered them in the garden she had grown and tended to for five years.

***

David Aaronson spent the following month enveloped in work, becoming a man of many cases and many papers, abandoning the man that had once shared the life with Susan. He found comfort in the after-work routine of accompanying Latham to the King's Head Pub downtown.

On the television one night was an update on the Wilcox trial. The pub's TV was perpetually muted, so they couldn't hear a word.

"I spoke to the prosecutor," Latham said, eyes glazed at the screen. "Apparently defense is going for the insanity plea. No other real way they could go. She fully admits to what she did, but doesn't claim guilt in anything."

"What she did wasn't wrong," said Aaronson. "To her."

"Well, yeah, of course. It never is to people like that…" He gave an exaggerated shiver as he took a sip of Newcastle. "Really can't get over it, you know?"

"What?"

"How someone like Allison Wilcox will probably end up taking up space at some monkey house for another sixty years, while someone like Susan …"

"Don't worry about it, Richard. I know. Believe me, I know."

"I'm sorry, Dave."

Aaronson didn't respond, only idly read the beer label as he picked at it.

Latham asked, "How many have you had?"

"Enough," he said, and stumbled off the stool.

***

Normally after a sufficient amount of alcohol, David Aaronson could lie down and be turned off as effortlessly as a lamp, but that night—along with all previous nights since the fourteenth—thoughts of Susan banished sleep.

He tried to read. He watched television. He cooked a

midnight snack, then realized he wasn't hungry. It was all in an effort to not look at the photos, the three albums of his life with Susan that sat on the bottom of the living room bookshelf.

Then something crept into his brain. He picked up the phone.

He sat and stared for a long time, engaged in a disjointed showdown with his own curiosity. He shifted the cell phone from hand to hand, like a hot potato, afraid of what might happen if it stayed in one palm too long, there being nothing left to do but press the keys, to begin dialing...

...1...

...1...

...1...

Stop.

The screen was lit, bearing its newly input teeth of three ones. One more. Why was this so damn difficult? This thing was all bullshit anyway.

In a crashing second he became blind and deaf with adrenaline and pressed once more.

...1. *Send*.

Slowly he lifted the phone to his ear, part of him expecting (and a huge part of him praying) to hear the harsh chimes of a misdialed or non-existent number, to have the pleasantly soulless recording tell him as such.

In his mind he saw Susan on the hospital bed, seconds beyond life.

Then it began to ring.

Community

…and he tore through the brush, the world pushing against him, the wet maw of the creature no more than two feet behind him. His pursuer was snorting and he couldn't tell if it was from waning energy or the renewed urging of a desperate hunger.

He moved fast, but so did the beast, and when he was no more than five feet from shelter the giant thing knew of its imminent failure and lashed out, snapping its jaws into a gnarled, thorny bush. He could feel the expelled breath of blood and meat, the death-stain that had yellowed all its teeth.

Racing into his shelter, he was invisible. The pursuer snorted in frustration and lumbered away. It was the fifth one of those things he'd outrun that week, and he wondered how much more luck nature had in store for him.

His feet throbbed, outspoken ambassadors for the rest of his body that beat and pulsed and shivered. He needed to calm himself and try and live through another night without enough food.

He hated those things out there, the beasts that roamed the sun-baked lands. They all ranged greatly in size—some were unspeakably large, but those he didn't have to worry about. Their heads touched the sky, and they would never notice him.

It was the much smaller ones he had to fear. The ones that could easily spot him and, in one sweeping gulp, mangle his furry insignificance into nothing. That was why he hid from the sun-baked lands, why he'd carved his own little hole of nighttime in which to feel warm, safe, protected.

Soon, exhaustion cleansed the heat of the encounter. He nibbled on some of the pickings he'd managed to scrounge on a previous nocturnal food run.

As he nestled himself in to sleep, he thought how he should never set foot into the sun-baked lands, how daylight should never see his snout again. Not until it was safe. Not until they were all dead.

This thought pleased him, and he rode it off into a dream.

crawling—crumbling—snorting
—gnashing—

Death had plowed its way into his shelter, exploding him from his sleep. The long, scaly snout repeated its pattern of withdrawing and charging, hammering more open space in which to move and spread its jaws even further.

He scurried to the back of his shelter and squealed, squealed for help, squealed to leave his last mark in the listening ears of the community around him.

His final cry was heard among the region, but all remained silent as the beast moved away with its late-afternoon meal between its teeth.

Another had died.

At a distant level, the rest of the community knew it was only a matter of time before the fear would be over. It was an elusive notion, but it had flesh, it was tangible. Some faint promise on the wind. Maybe it would happen soon. There would always be bigger things out there, but if they could hold out just long enough, perhaps they would have the privilege of walking the dry sun-baked lands unscathed and unafraid.

Perhaps one day they could claim the world.

The following morning, a brilliant light colored the sky, and descended toward the mountain range far to the east.

The Cyclops Conference

"Come with me, I'm going to show you where my eyes are."

The man with the sunglasses, the blind man called Gene Wallathorp who'd owned and worked Jacksboro's Swirling Colors Ice Cream Parlor for as long as Barbara Mendez could remember, was suddenly a stranger to her. He'd always been a bit off-kilter, but it wasn't his blindness—that was merely one swollen cloud against a gathering storm.

In her twenty years of coming here, ever since bouncing in as a freshly tonsil-less eight-year-old, Barbara had never seen Gene's eyes. Yet the man often moved with intuitive grace, the rest of his body projecting a body language that was authoritative, in control. He wasn't bothered by his blindness, and wouldn't allow his customers to be, either. Newcomers were often treated to his impressive memory of the precise location of all twenty arrayed flavors.

Yes, always odd. Today, however, Barbara had no idea what he was talking about.

"Excuse me, Gene?" she said, licking a clump of mint chip from her cone. "Your eyes?"

"Yes, Barbara, my eyes. I've found them. I never in a million years could've believed such a thing to happen. As

139

far as I know, it's never even happened before. But they've stopped moving and I've found them—all of them."

"Mr. Wallathorp, what in Christ's name are you talking about? You're scaring me."

Gene paced back and forth, bobbing with excitement. "I'm going to close up shop early today. Come with me? Please come with me, Barbara. You've been one of my most faithful customers. I remember when you were just a little girl, so tender, asking your mother quietly what was wrong with me and why I wore these glasses all the time. But I could hear you, and hear you well—nature never takes away without giving. And now… it has given back to me my eyes."

"Please, Mr. Wallathorp…"

"I'm not conventionally blind, Barbara," Gene said, pinching the frames of his sunglasses in preparation to remove them.

Something of a curious panic stirred within her.

"I don't have eyes—period."

He removed the glasses, revealing two black sockets like that of a skeleton's, caverns that led a promising yet ultimately dead-end route to the brain beyond Gene's skull.

"Oh… my God."

"I don't want to frighten you." Gingerly he placed the glasses back on his head. "But I am thrilled because I won't have to look like this anymore. I can recover. I can be normal once more. And I want you to share this with me."

"What?"

"Please. For obvious reasons, I can't drive there myself."

"Drive where?" Barbara was about to say she had to meet

someone, but lying to this man, a prominent town figure, suddenly seemed futile.

"Just drive me to the conference, north of town in the hills," Gene said. "I can guide you. Please." His voice wasn't so much pleading as it was pleasantly commanding, very much in line with the subtle dominance Gene often held over people with whom he would interact. Barbara had felt it when she was eight, standing there with a throat gutted of tonsils. She still felt it now, that authoritative confidence that brought both respect for him and had enflamed her teenage desire to rebel against him. During high school, she'd become a thieving pro at plucking money from his register and the charity jar.

"How do you know where this thing is?" she asked Gene, suddenly wary and sick of the ice cream in her hand. She wanted to shove it in his face and run, but remained still. Why? Guilt? No, he hadn't suspected anything, the poor bastard was blind, after all, and truth be told she hadn't been that desperate for money in a long while.

"I know where it is," Gene said, grin spreading, "because my eyes are there."

***

"Where are we going, Mr. Wallathorp?"

They'd left Jacksboro, traveling along the road curving listlessly into the patchy fields and hills. Once they were immersed in woods, Gene began to speak.

"It's what they call a Cyclops conference," he said, "because it looks like one giant eye, kind of. Supposedly. I don't know, I've never seen it before. Frankly, I thought it was just a story they told to give people with my condition some faint ray of hope."

"Your condition?"

"Yes. I lost my eyes about thirty years ago, when they matured enough to leave their home in my sockets. They just up and left one night, popping out and scuttling on their own merry way. And, according to what I've been told, the eyes meet every ten years in these conferences, thousands of them, to mate or to feed, I'm not quite sure…"

"You're telling me your eyes are…living things?"

"I am. It's a rare condition. They even have their own species name but I can't remember it, name's really long. But for a while they lived in my skull, and I fed them. I fed them the world, but once they reached a certain age they wanted to sate their own appetites, to see it for themselves."

"You're crazy, and I'm calling the police," she said, going for her cell phone.

"Just hold on, Barbara," Gene said, feeling for her and calmly placing his hand on her arm. "I know it sounds like I've lost my marbles. Trust me, I haven't. You're about to witness a rare and marvelous spectacle, and, once I find my eyes, I'll be able to partake in the experience with you."

"I thought you could see where they are and what they were doing."

"Not like you can, or anyone else can. It's more like a sixth sense, a phantom limb kind of connection I have with them."

He smiled.

Barbara was eight years old and scared of him again. She gripped the steering wheel tighter and pressed the accelerator harder. The car complained but found its strength and made headway up the mountain, where hearty pines stood dense and towering.

"There! Turn here!"

Gene was jamming his finger left and Barbara swerved the vehicle in the desired direction. Tires raked the pavement. They rolled onto a dirt path, long disused and slowly being entombed by creeping weeds and shrubbery.

In moments they reached a clearing.

"I can hear them," Gene said. "I can hear them. Stop the car, we can walk from here."

"Mr. Wallathorp—"

"Shhh." He opened the door and climbed out, cane ready in hand. "Just follow me. Toward the sounds. Can you hear that?"

Barbara strained to listen, but all she could hear was the wind in the trees, and the frequent call of what sounded like a raven. Gene fumbled for her hand, found it before she could react and led her across a path of sounds only he could hear.

Then it was there, spread upon her vision like spilt reality.

There had to be thousands of eyes, bunched together and moving, bubbling and mingling with one another as they whispered their sights and experiences untold. Barbara thought they looked like giant maggots. Eager to settle her stomach, she went bounding behind the nearest tree, but she could still hear them, could still hear the eyes as they slithered over the ground and one another.

On the other side of the clearing was a young boy helping an older man with sunglasses retrieve his eyes. The boy knelt ankle-deep in the pool of retinas and corneas, scouring the conference until finally plucking two eyeballs from it.

"I think I've found them, Grampa!" she heard the boy shout. "I've found 'em!"

Meanwhile, Gene was in awe. He took cautious strides towards the swarm.

"Find me, kids," he said. "Find me. Come home."

Barbara took a deep breath and made herself peer around the tree. Gene stood still, arms outstretched, impersonating the classic Biblical image. Hundreds of dry eyes crawled in true cockroach fashion amongst his shoes, covering most of them, some inching up his left sock towards his pant leg. They hissed, somehow, and buzzed. They swarmed and huddled. Finally a pair separated from the mass and made their way up the outside of Gene's pants, past his belt and towards his face. The two eyeballs were close to one another, hurriedly dragging their optic nerve tails in the nostalgic spirit of reunion.

The eyeballs crawled up Gene's cheeks, one on each side of his nose, and found his gaping sockets, and it was there they nestled, squirming and squiggling to find the best fit, much as a large man might in a small chair. Then Gene blinked, and they were again as one.

Barbara stood motionless and cold with disbelieving horror. Gene turned toward her. Across the field, the older man led his grandson away from the conference.

"I'm afraid I sort of, hmm, how should I say, bent the

truth a little," Gene said, approaching her now, vision fully intact. With his finished face Barbara was astounded at how different he looked —for years the sunglasses had always seemed like a missing puzzle piece, a dark hole that needed patching, and while she often imagined what he'd look like with working eyes, she never thought he'd be this striking.

"My eyes didn't run away," he said. "I let them loose. I don't have a condition—I have an ability. I imagine spies and stalkers would give up their left arms for such a talent."

Barbara started backing up, but with each step of hers, Gene took two—she couldn't get away from him fast enough.

"I set my eyes free, Barbara. Like loyal dogs they roam the neighborhood of my associates, acquaintances and friends, swallowing their lives and thus laying the eggs of their sights into my brain once I retrieved them, here, at the hub of this conference. And I must say… I am quite stunned by what a reprobate person you've become."

"What the hell are you *talking* about, you fucking freak cripple?"

"Your two marriages, ruined by affairs… cheating your way through school… running over Ms. Lewis' cat and never telling her… stealing money from my cash register since you were fifteen, all the while thinking my handicap was your perfect cover." Gene spat on the ground. "You're a disgrace, Barbara, and I've watched every minute of it. I've been on the walls, behind the dresser, under your car seat… all around you."

A ripping sense of violation tore through Barbara. She

felt queasy. Behind Gene, the mass bubbling of the eyeball gathering buzzed and hissed.

"You've been watching me... invading me..." Nails hammered her chest. "You're just as disgusting, you freak!"

"Just drive me back," Gene said. "Drive me back to my shop."

They climbed into the car, Barbara breathing heavily, shuddering. She dropped the keys and screamed, apologized, then shoved them into the ignition. She was drained and humiliated, as though she'd been pinned up naked for the world to mock and judge and accuse.

She drove in silence, cemented in the driver's seat, not daring to look at Gene next to her. The forest sped past them, the town of Jacksboro waiting below, sprawled across the terrain like, like...

The images of all the eyeballs hit her again. The town at the base of the mountain, blinking hundreds of lights in the coming dusk, now reminded her of Gene's Cyclops conference.

Barbara tried to remain still, to not look at him. She could feel him looking in her direction, the shadow of his face in the corner of her eye. She felt like he was smiling, relishing having torn open and exposed the broken anatomy of her life, her secrets.

There was a fleeting movement when, out of frightened instinct, she glanced at Gene, who sat looking at her now with only one eye. The other socket was black and empty, missing its occupant.

Then she felt something on her arm, scuttling up across

her shoulder and tickling the open skin on the back of her neck.

"Always know, Barbara..." Gene said, turning back to the window, "...that I will always... *always*... keep my eye on you."

Trail

"So you're definitely not coming tomorrow?" Thomas Roland asked his partner.

Eric Baron lined up his shot and struck the cue ball. It sailed to the right, defying the intended aim and rolling and bouncing in the green negative space among the balls. Not wanting to watch the scratch, he looked up at Thomas.

"No, I'd better not," Eric said.

"Still feeling it, eh?"

"Yeah, it's been a little better the past day or so, but this past week it's felt like something's taken a big bite out of my energy. Just felt weak. I think I'm fighting something off."

"Mmm."

The Bee Gees sang from the jukebox, their high nasal lyrics poking at the soft murmuring tissue of conversation that now grew across Friday night at Roy's House of Billiards. The lights dimmed and balls knocked and clattered against each other in rainbow chaos.

Tom stood over his shot, lined it up. "So I guess I'm not hitting any trails this week, either?"

"Why not? Go ahead. Don't need me."

"It's a better time with two people. You know that."

Having met in college, the two men had built a relationship largely around their love for the outdoors. *Nature was our matchmaker*, went their favorite line. Since moving in together they'd taken to ritual hikes in the Santa Monica Mountain range, the swath of backcountry dividing Los Angeles. And when work was particularly trying, or the pull of nature particularly urgent, they often drove an hour or two north, past the county line to the forests and hills of an easy-breathing California.

"How long have you been feeling like this?" Tom asked. "Seems like it's been a while."

"Like five days. If it goes on another week, I'm going to see the doctor, but I think it's going away." Holding his cue vertical, Eric pounded the floor softly with the thick end. "What got me irritated was that I started feeling weak when I found that trail, so I couldn't go much further."

"Yeah, still went long enough to run into that bobcat," Tom said.

"Hey, you were the one that chose to have Mommy time. I can't help it if I need to get my nature fix. I'll do it alone if I have to."

"Sure you can help it. If my mom can now resist a drink, you can hold off on the beautiful trails and wild animals until I'm around."

Eric struck a solid ball that hit the corner of a pocket and ricocheted back and forth before deciding not to drop in.

"Son of a bitch."

"That's what you get," Tom said, moving around the table. From the jukebox The Beatles now sang *Yellow*

Submarine. "How about you wake up tomorrow and see how you feel."

"Sure."

"I mean, I don't even know where this trail is. How did you find it?"

"It literally just popped out at me. I was driving down Pacific Coast Highway about five miles from the county line and there it was, this opening into this canyon that I'd completely missed."

"Wait, had you already gone hiking beforehand?"

"Yeah, up on the Chumash Trail. I took the scenic route."

"Well, no wonder you were exhausted."

Eric shrugged, nodding. "I suppose so."

Tom hit a striped ball into the middle pocket. "Does the trail have a name, do you know?"

"I honestly couldn't tell you. I didn't see any sign with any names. That was actually kind of the charm."

Tom nodded. "So you're gonna tell me where this place is, right?"

"Of course," Eric said. "I'll point you in the general vicinity. You just have to keep your eyes open."

"Sure you don't want to come with me?"

"I want to, you know that, but I'm afraid whatever I've got will just drag you down. Go see it for yourself."

Eric knocked in his first ball of the night, a solid two, and Tom checked his watch, now anticipating an early rise for the hike the following morning.

***

His alarm chimed at six. The sound woke Eric, yet only enough for him to croak out a half-conscious farewell and roll over back to sleep. Tom gathered himself and his things—most of which he'd packed the night before after returning from Roy's—whispered his own farewell and was out the door to meet the weekend morning.

Thomas Roland loved Pacific Coast Highway, the long, calligraphic stroke of pavement tracing this westernmost part of the country. With the glistening plane of the ocean constantly on the left, the drive was pretty through the more urban areas of Santa Monica and Malibu, but didn't really get dancing for Tom until the limit sign for L.A. County was about a mile behind him.

He reached the Chumash Trail, one he and Eric had taken numerous times, supposedly near the spot that had "popped out" at his partner. He drove for several miles along the highway. Beyond a handful of cars there was nothing but large palisades of stone and sand. He tried to peer in close, much as driving almost sixty along a curvy highway would allow, but saw nothing—no inlets, no canyons or crevices where a little Eden might be hiding.

An hour after sunrise, Thomas Roland thought he had finally discovered the entrance—just east of Malibu—to the "paradise" described by Eric.

He parked along the side of the road and unloaded his gear, strapped on his backpack, rechecked his water supply, ensuring everything was in place. He trudged up the hill past the craggy earth and large brown stones and entered the small, almost vaginal opening in the canyon where beyond the dusty sighs of sand and wind there stretched a place of striking green beauty.

The woods were pulsing, resplendent with life, great spidery webs of branches and foliage glittering in the daylight. The outside world: banished. Large boulders jutted from the ground, ringed by eyelashes of grass. As Tom moved past them, he saw flickers of movement in the nooks and cracks, felt the phantom weight of eyes on him. He kept walking, then stopped when his eyes met that of a bobcat's perched on a rock.

"Oh my God."

For a good moment he stared at the cat, then pulled out his cell phone. Still had enough reception. He dialed. After two rings Eric's sleepy voice came on the line.

"Hey," said Tom.

"What's wrong?" Eric said. "Did you find the trail okay?"

"No, not the one you were telling me about. But I found a trail that's probably just as good if not better. And get this, I'm about twenty feet from a bobcat right now."

"Really?"

"Yeah, he's perched on a big rock, just to the left of the trail. Big guy, too."

"Perched on a rock?" repeated Eric. "What color is he? Light brown?"

"Yeah…"

"Is he eyeing something on the ground?"

Tom looked towards the grass at the base of the rock. A small flutter of movement. Two rabbit ears sticking into view. He followed the sight up to the hungry green eyes of the bobcat.

"He's looking at a rabbit."

There was a haunted pause on the other end.

"My bobcat was scoping out a rabbit, too," he said, hesitantly. "Think it might be the same one?"

"Really? That's... funny," Tom said, feeling strange. "Listen, I'm gonna head on up a bit further, but I'll be back before noon."

Perhaps figuring Tom might also be after the rabbit and in no mood for competition, the cat slunk away behind the rock and into the forest.

Tom hung up and continued hiking. A quarter mile in, a subtle tiredness crept into his bones, moving stealthily, eddying through his arms and legs. Part of him wanted to stop, to turn around as Eric had, but the magnetic wonder of this decidedly non-L.A. trail was addicting—like a child always wanting one more candy. Tom wanted just another step, then another. Another.

Half a mile in, breath came hard. He was slightly dizzy. He slowed, head down. A queer claustrophobic sensation took him—the woods were narrowing, aiming to constrict. Encroaching closer, closer.

Tom snapped his head up. Nothing had moved.

What is wrong with me?

He had to go back. Walking was now like slogging across great dunes of soft sand. Every step counted for three. He turned, reversed direction, then realized the flanking trees and rocks were unfamiliar, though the trail itself looked unchanged. Panic built in his chest.

What the hell?

A veteran hiker, Tom always made conscious effort to drop mental breadcrumbs along every trail he took. And really, such an exercise was only necessary if the trail branched off or forked, or somehow took a winding, confusing tangent. Such was not the case with this trail, which was fairly linear and had only taken moderate turns.

From the shrubbery just beyond a fallen sycamore he heard a voice, barely audible. Tom could pick up no words, but the sound was pained, borderline moaning. He summoned enough energy to explore.

"Hello?" he called.

The voice stopped.

He pressed on, shoving aside the brush that snapped defiantly back into place. Heart racing, Tom no longer felt his legs.

(—heart attack—stroke—embolism—)

In the brush was a man, fallen near a cactus patch. He was old—extremely old, almost cartoonishly so, his skin like weathered dried fruit, cilia of creases on his flat centipede lips.

"Can you hear me?" Tom asked. "Sir?"

Jesus.

The old man was dead. Upon inspection Tom saw a bulge in the man's back pocket and pulled out a wallet. Numerous cards. Memberships. Credit. Business. A little over twenty-five dollars cash.

And the license.

The man, whose name was John Maddock, was only thirty-two years old. Yet the prostrate form at Tom's feet couldn't have been under eighty.

Tom got out his cell phone. No service. He prodded Maddock with his foot, called his name. Nothing.

Slowly he moved away from the area, the haunting, exhausted throb now a painful ache hindering him. He thought of Eric, where his trail was, wishing he were there now. Wishing he were anywhere else.

Maybe I am there.

Whether desperate for answers or desperate to assert itself against this frightening and seemingly irrational situation, Tom's brain heaped up scattered memories, one of which, very recent, stood out: his partner Eric, holding vertical his pool cue, remarking, "What got me irritated was that I started feeling weak when I found that trail, so I couldn't go much further."

Felt weak, Tom thought.

It nibbled at him.

Took from him.

He closed his eyes. *No, no, that's impossible... fucking impossible...*

Maybe it... moved...

Stop.

...moved like any predator would into better position....

Goddammit, no—

...to strike.

Small mammals bounded under shrubs into the ground. The birds unleashed synchronous cries. Unseen larger animals gave their own cries. The treetops were a bristly moving sculpture of wind.

Tom fell to his knees, wholly drained, the minutes, hours, days, weeks, months, years of all tomorrows siphoned steadily from his marrow into the thousand-rooted throats of these wilds—sating, rejuvenating, every flower, plant, tree, and rock.

The wind continued its wordless murmur, the only sound now.

Spooklights

The town of Lansboro had many names for them. They called them fireflies at first, with a reluctant voice tremor that always indicated it was merely a familiar nickname—you know, to offset the phenomenon's decided *un*familiarity. Then they were labeled meteors, or asteroids, or ball lightning.

Lansboro had seen meteor showers before and was rational enough to know the lights were no meteors or asteroids or fireflies. It also had its share of stars at night, a glittering dome framed by the full, dark Pennsylvania woods cupping the town, the scattered lights of which were a pale reflection of the twinkling party far above.

Someone said that, too, that these lights were having a party.

The first time I saw them they were darting across the sky, slitting open the dark as they zipped right to left, bouncing around in a chaotic repertoire, drawing parabolas and circles and looking like massive lost electrons whipping around, seeking an atom to orbit.

I was out in the backyard the fourth time they came—since June they had been occurring monthly, at roughly the same time each time, too. I watched from the grass as the lights played in the sky. George, my father more or less, was inside the darkened trailer, the television flashing its own light in the small, grimy window that looked out on the yard. I felt safer out here, ironically, more at home—once perceived as an ominous threat, the lights had become more an anticipated spectacle.

Part of their beauty was in the multicolored afterimages they left on my retinas, globs of blue when they hovered, erratic ribbons of white and green when they moved fast, zipping along with double the ability of a water snake through a pond.

The afterimage colors were the first thing I remembered *remembering*. I had never really seen anything like them before, and if I had, it sure hadn't left it mark the way these lights had.

Behind me Ms. Mackey's trailer door creaked open, then clapped shut with an echo. Inside, I saw her dog Tyler on the floor, droopy head supported by two paws. Mackey staggered towards me, smiling behind a cigarette she was trying to light. I hated cigarettes—the smell was downright awful, and if that wasn't enough, George would occasionally chuck dying ones at me while I was resting. Lately he had realized he could get away with such things now that Mom was gone.

"They are quite beautiful, aren't they, Cleveland?" said Ms. Mackey, cigarette successfully lit.

Ms. Mackey was a decent woman—often times she would give me the love or the food needed whenever George decided that I didn't exist, which was often. I'd learned to make do on my own sometimes, but independence, and true confidence in that independence, had yet to settle into my bones.

"You wonder about them, don't you?" Ms. Mackey said, entranced. "I look at these lights and I feel like I'm being invited to some kind of… oh I don't know, some kind of heavenly celebration."

The spooklights—a name that still clung to Lansboro's tongue even though hardly anyone was ever really spooked any more—were by now four months old. When they first came, no one would leave their homes or trailers. The zipping spheres left Lansboro bathed in an eerie yellow-orange glow that didn't pulse to the movement of the lights, but remained constant. It was like one massive porch light, illuminating everything within several miles.

They made no noise, strangely enough, preferring only to treat the eyes. And it was because of this that many in town, myself included, initially thought them hallucinations. I think everyone at one point or another mistook them as vision spots, or symptoms of some neurological disease.

Ms. Mackey kept smoking, inhaling, exhaling. She'd stopped talking, thankfully. I kept silent.

The lights continued their luminescent ballet. Others had since trickled outside to watch them, some having even set up folding chairs atop their trailers to take it all in. It was a testament to how accustomed to them the town had become, treating it with the acceptance of Fourth of July fireworks.

That was first time I remember feeling cold, too. The

night was cold. I had felt this sensation before, of course, numerous times—but that night the feeling emerged from a fog in my memory as a clearly defined and much more potent entity, a searing presence.

Then something unusual happened. One of the lights broke off from the group and trailed downward, drawing a thin, bumpy path over the dark like a glow-in-the-dark lie detector. The ball on the end of the trail pulsed, like a heartbeat. Faint light cascaded over Lansboro. The cold loosened its bite.

"What is it doing?" Ms. Mackey said with a frightful tremor. "Is it coming down to us? Is it an angel?"

With my depth perception all out of whack in regards to the lights, I was unable to tell if they were directly over the Lansboro woods, or simply large orbs hovering further away on the horizon.

"It's never come to the ground before, has it, Cleveland?"

There was something irrational in Ms. Mackey's face. Normally a woman of calm yet formidable strength, Ms. Mackey that night appeared distracted—loopy. I recognized her shaky voice, her trembling cigarette passed from trembling hand to trembling lips, and her eyes, her eyes, the jittery motions of her pupils, each ephemeral movement a capricious thought.

In many ways she reminded me of myself. Maybe that's how I recognized it so fast.

"Hey! Cleveland! Come on back in 'ere!" George shouted from the door of the trailer, where from inside the television continued flashing blue seizures.

I called back to George in a low, protesting voice, but knew I'd have to go back. Many times I'd had the instinct to run away, but I think it was the ghost of Mom's presence that kept me there, a suspicion that I'd be betraying her memory if I were to leave, even though I was sure she'd understand. I would find the courage she never could.

George quite disliked me, but for some odd reason didn't want to get rid of me. He would regularly pounce on anyone, like Ms. Mackey, who threatened to give me a better home. I think the obligation to Mom was strong enough to influence even a beast like him.

"What's going on?" George craned his head skyward, where the spooklights, after their usual twenty-minute run, were beginning to slink back into the darkness like crumbs dissolving in water, always a rather anticlimactic finale to their inspiring dance.

"It's the lights again," said George. He looked at me. "Cleveland, get back in here. Now."

I obliged.

"Bye, Cleveland," Ms. Mackey said. I didn't turn around.

George gave me a little boot through the door, then let it slam shut as he hurried off to bathroom. I took my spot on the other side of the trailer and stared out at what I could see of Lansboro—the other trailers, two of them lit, one still sporting holiday decorations. Rising above them like a frozen tsunami was the forest, a wall of blackness defined only by the absence of stars.

George returned from the bathroom and resumed his seat in front of the television.

"What's with all this hip-hop crap?" he muttered, clicking the remote. "Loud-mouthed black music all over the place."

I had no idea what he was talking about. I didn't care. I just snuggled up on my bed, eased my body into the cushion around the dead cigarette butts. Once I fell asleep, I had a dream that I was someone, someone in Lansboro. I walked around outside, chatting with people like Ms. Mackey. Her dog sat by her side, and the dog spoke, strangely enough, with sophisticated eloquence.

The dream waned as I awoke. I was, however, able to retain various morsels of it, and through the following day it stuck with me, something that had never happened before.

***

That September, George quit his construction job and spent much of his days in the trailer, eating cereal out of the box and devoting more time to fixing, rather than watching, the television.

We tried ignoring each other. One time he caught me in a wide-eyed daydream, my gaze seemingly focused on him.

"What're you looking at, Cleveland?" he said.

I placed my head back down, wanting to sleep but suddenly recognizing my desperate hunger. I let George know, but after four tries all I received was a harsh "Shut up."

You're going to die.

I stopped—or rather, my brain stopped.

(Die? Death?)

What did that mean? It meant the end. If I was going to die, that was it. The end.

George can die, can't he?

Of course he can.

I made do by scavenging on the crumbs of food littering trailer, as well as taking the insects that had come for the very same thing.

***

The spooklights came again the following month, right on schedule, performing their roller-coaster ballet in the night sky.

It was the night Ms. Mackey had trouble speaking.

It was also the night I began to notice the fur on my arms.

***

Sometime—I think it was in the middle of autumn—the whole town changed.

Kids appeared the most affected. They had all been transformed into creatures and animals, or mangled, nightmarish versions of themselves. They roamed outside, approaching the doors of each trailer, carrying what looked like bags. I didn't watch for long, and at that moment I was thoroughly glad of George's voluntary isolation, because he left the trailer dark, which seemed to deter the transformed children. They assumed it was unoccupied.

What is happening? To Lansboro? To them? To me?

— spooklights –

George ended up going out at nights, probably to a new job. He would dress in a uniform, be gone from about mid-evening to sunrise, and come back and watch television or snack in his usual spot until falling asleep. I didn't mind the change, particularly, as it diminished his presence all night and virtually all day, but that night I didn't like being left alone. Something was going on. Something was wrong. All sorts of creatures milled about outside, one of them even coming around and checking out our trailer, inside which I remained dead still, careful not to give any indication of my presence.

Sometime just before George returned, they all died down, and I was able to get some sleep.

It was at the blackest of night, the epicenter of darkness… that I awoke and noticed my tail.

***

I soon realized how much I slept during the day—and night, too. Ironically, while George also slept often, he would still badger me about not doing anything. Such outbursts, however, were usually drunken, and, I suspected, more from frustration and jealousy than anything else.

I suppose such revelations had been in me prior, but I had never really known them until that fourth spooklight month (that's how I came to start telling time, from the lights). In fact, the world itself seemed to be waking up for me—it glowed brighter, smelled fresher and it was more *there*, its presence strong.

I admitted to myself that, although I couldn't do the kinds of things George did, I certainly did spend much of my life unconscious. Once, it seemed necessary to keep my body and my muscles relaxed and tender. Now it struck me as a waste.

What was out there?

Or heck, what was in *here*? In Lansboro? I hadn't ever been out much, mostly because of Mom's worries—she had been especially concerned about Ms. Mackey's dog, Tyler, but he seemed just as jailed as I.

To quell this urge for the outdoors, I tried distracting myself. I tried turning on the television, but found it too frustrating an ordeal, too clumsy as I was in touch and height to do it properly. And you could forget about changing channels.

Begrudgingly, I returned to my corner, tried to sleep. But now there was a mental block there. Once able to shut everything off with the pull of a singular bodily switch, I found it had since been broken into a panel of thousands of switches. My mind raced, stirring with some new life. It would do no good to try resting on such a hotbed of energy.

I needed to get out.

***

The next month the lights came again, their sixth showing, and this time I saw Ms. Mackey engaged in a most bizarre activity: she was squatting on the grass, looking curiously at a raccoon ambling away from her. This month, she didn't even seem to notice the lights, staring instead at the raccoon as though she'd never seen one before. He was the usual chap, though, this raccoon. He'd come around often to scrounge through the trash bins.

The critter was calm and unfazed as Mackey rested her knuckles on the ground. At one point, the raccoon's burglar-mask eyes hit me dead-on as I sat and watched from the window—

What is Ms. Mackey doing?

—and we connected, in a sense I cannot explain, not even today. But it was something I had never felt before. An unknown weight swelled in me.

Ms. Mackey began sniffing the grass. I left my perch at the window. George would be back any minute. I had become more aware of "smaller time" now—beginning with vague milestones marked by the spooklights, I'd soon become aware of the shorter units of days, hours, minutes.

I was acutely aware, however, of the time I looked at Mom's old cross on the wall, noticed the message written on it. The word LORD popped out suddenly, and it took me a few seconds to gather myself and realize what had just happened.

I had *read*.

***

The trailer grew more foul and disgusting in the following month. George stopped using the bathroom and simply went wherever he felt. He even befouled my designated place to go, to the point where I myself had no choice but to follow suit.

I went in a frying pan, for both functions.

George's speech was noticeably scarred, too, and I wondered if he'd had some accident at his night job. Until I remembered Ms. Mackey's language mishaps the previous month, how she would slur every other word or so, and the stuttering that I'd never before heard from her.

As the days and weeks went by, readable words came easier. I read SONY on the television, I could discern the word "charms" on a cereal box, and by the end of a solid week of practice, of clarity, I was able to read the entire passage on Mom's old cross.

Oh Lord, give me the strength, the will, the mind, to face the new day.

It was an amusing hobby, and it preoccupied me, kept my mind afloat. After spending a week on single words, I soon found myself able to grasp whole sentences, then paragraphs, and actually took stimulating pleasure in dragging out what decrepit books of Mom's remained in the nooks of the trailer and reading them. Handling the books required finesse quite foreign to me, but I trained myself, dedicating much of my energies to turning the pages.

My theory is that, having been around people's language my entire life, my own language abilities had been lying dormant, deep within me. Yet whatever was going on in these months— whatever was happening to me—had summoned the words to the surface, as surely as rain flushed worms from the soil.

One time I saw a mouse poking about in a Lucky Charms box left half-empty on the floor, his little stringy tail jutting from the open flap.

I moved in closer, my shoulders hunched, trying not to make much noise. I was hungry again, and peered inside. The creature was as big as my two front paws combined (paws, paws, yes that's what they are called), and he nibbled furiously on a Lucky Charms morsel, his whole body

169

shivering with each bite, his eyes little black balls of dead-set business.

But there was more to him.

He saw me. We both froze. Something stayed my attack. Something overrode my hunger.

I let out a small noise. The mouse responded with little wet squeaks.

I had an idea. Atop the counter were more open cereal boxes. George liked to try new kinds, or maybe he just hated each new one he got and would try another. Either way, the purchases of numerous brands of cereal would now come in handy, provided there was enough Alphabet Crunch left.

Springing myself onto the counter, I rummaged around the dishes, the wrappers and the boxes and found the box I was looking for. I shoved it towards the edge, batted it around a few other obstacles, then sent it over. The mouse remained still, transfixed. Probably wondering what I was doing, debating whether or not to make a scurrying escape.

Striking the floor, the box spewed a rainbow gibberish of letters across the carpet. The mouse recoiled, squeaking again, but didn't run away. Instead, it put down its mangled Lucky Charm and emerged cautiously into better light.

We met gazes as I hopped back down beside the Alphabet Crunch. I stood relaxed, ears up, trying to assuage his fears, to appear non-threatening. The small creature seemed to understand.

Sifting through the cereal, I found four of the letters I wanted, but couldn't find an H. Figuring one must be in the box with the fragmented pieces, I batted it and pushed it up with my snout, trying to get it at an angle so that more might pour out.

The mouse, however, seemed to have a solution. When I looked over he had maneuvered two Is in front of the ELLO I had laid out. Then he placed the remnant crumb of his Lucky Charms meal between them, so it looked something like this:

⊣ELLO

I vocalized my greeting the best way I knew, and the tiny rodent squeaked again, bobbing his head rapidly. The same connection I'd felt with the raccoon was evident here, too. That sense of knowing. That heated awareness that there was another like you. That there were, perhaps, untold numbers of those like you. Innumerable minds, all separate, all unique, each holding a piece of the answer sought by all.

Then, there was another side of me that wanted to eat this piece of answer.

The trailer door suddenly shuddered, cutting our little encounter short. The mouse darted away into unseen places. I backed up, watching the door. George came bursting in, uniform tattered. I leapt onto the armchair of the couch, ready. On guard.

"Flee mos ran uk," George said.

He can't speak he can't speak—

George staggered through the trailer, destructive energies centered mostly on the kitchen area. I ran across the couch and alighted on his bed. He lumbered past me, simian arms swinging low and wide.

Perched on his bed, I watched him, spine shivering.

"Cllvand watchu neem man!" he shouted.

George lunged for me and I deftly evaded his meaty grasping hands. How did I do that? As I'd always done, I realized. Only now I *knew* I'd done it. In me had grown a kind of detached spectator. A mind.

Watching him from atop one of the kitchen cabinets, the roof of the trailer only inches above me, I warned George not to try anything. I warned him to back away. The warnings came not as words, however—my physiology didn't know words. So I hissed, flattened my ears. The rough texture of my tongue grazed something in my mouth, something wet, and hard, sharp.

Fangs. I've got fangs.

Realization of myself—what I was, what I possessed— now filled me. Small tremors shook in various places of my body. There was something pushing inside of me, parting old habits, demanding room for itself, a thing not new but old, always there but now simply elevated, highlighted. I could sense them now. I was aware of them, and aware of the awareness of being aware!

George stumbled about by the strings of utter terrified instinct. It almost felt like the more he let go, the more I gained.

He threw a strainer at me that hit the edge of the cabinet and tumbled onto the counter and back onto the floor, where it rolled a half circle and stopped at his feet. He shrieked—a high, agitated sound—and kicked it away. I hissed at him again, and felt something else this time.

My claws had come out, slid out from the trenches of my fur like straightened soldiers to perform their duty. George began hurling utensils my way, some of them knives, and I skittered across the cabinet top, tail brushing the ceiling, and leaped across the gap where the front door stood to the small bookshelf. I needed to find a way to open the door. Mom had never installed a special door for me, too afraid to let me go wandering in and out.

With one sweep of his right arm George cleared the kitchen counter. His skin now glistened with sweat, his jaw hung open. As he moved closer I readied myself. I would give him the last of the animal inside me. It was a test, a final exam before I could graduate to a higher self.

Ears flattened, tail down, claws out and fangs bared, I sprang myself with brutal accuracy onto George's face. Surprised, he cried out and stumbled back, his arms flailing to steady himself. I hooked my claws into his skin, anchoring myself as I dispatched my right claws into the warm, soft tissue of his eye. I dug, and I clutched, and I *tore*. George howled with pain.

I kept hissing as I clawed and bit his face. The bony top half of his nose was too hard to inflict much damage, but the cartilage of the lower half was easy on my teeth. His powerful hands grasped my back. The impact was heavy on my bones. A small bout of wind escaped me. I fell to the floor, shivering as one massive, furry nerve, my paws slimy with blood. George stumbled some more as I raced around the trailer, flying, jumping, like a frog on drugs, nothing he could ever contend with.

In screaming moans, face half-covered with a bloody hand, George groped towards the door. He pulled on it, right side gushing. When nothing happened, he started banging on it, hard, harder, knowing he knew how, but frustrated because he couldn't remember how to operate the knob.

Eventually it flew open with a *bang*. George stumbled out and fell to the grass, where there now walked, or crawled, a multitude of neighbors and Lansboro residents.

I slipped out the door and scooted around the trailer, almost running into a woman with dead eyes and searching arms. She grunted low, then hissed at me, snapping her head in a rapid fit. I darted between her legs and leapt onto a car several yards away, then made my way to the top of a nearby trailer where I sat and watched.

Primarily naked, the Lansboro residents now roamed the park, sniffing, tasting, hearing, touching the world anew. People emerged from their homes and their cars, their eyes fogged, their base motives clear. I watched them mate, I watched them fight. I watched them relieve themselves in arbitrary spots of the grass. I watched two of them toy with a milk snake under Ms. Mackey's trailer, swiping at it with grubby mitts, squatting and hopping, snorting in heated bewilderment.

From my perch I could see, or even sense, the presence of hundreds of other animals among Lansboro. They could sense me too, pets and wild ones alike. I wondered at the discrepancy between us and the wild ones, if language would come as easily to their minds, but it didn't matter at the time.

None of us had yet evolved any capacity for speech. We would perhaps connect with one another the way humans from two sides of the Pacific might have once connected.

***

The lights widened us, elevated us. I'm still uncertain as to the who, the how, and, most importantly, the why, or what—as in, what it wishes for us, or expects of us. Were only rodents and dogs, rabbits and raccoons, and felines like myself affected? Or will it be possible for me to run into a moose at some point and discuss Aristotle? Maybe talk of free will with a snake to get its mind off eating me?

To be honest, I'm not even sure the spooklights were responsible. But the theory fills two explanations, and it feels… *right.*

Our movement away from Lansboro became known, at least among those who participated in it, as the Great Migration. Factions of varying sizes moved in all directions from the town, expanding outwards. Who knew how many of us had been given the gift, if such a phenomenon was restricted to our little woodsy corner or if mammals the world over were awakening in their trees, holes, burrows, caves, and litter boxes to discover themselves and those around them.

I have no evidence that only mammals were affected, only a hunch.

I walked now with raccoons, mice, rats, squirrels, opossums, skunks, dozens of other cats and dogs in this Migration, and as we made our way through the forest we often happened upon new recruits more than glad to see they were not alone in this strange and sudden clarity.

Yet as we moved farther from Lansboro, the number of new encounters fell significantly. The forest became quiet, brush and canopy enclosing us. Many of us became tired and cold. Where were we going? What would we do?

I was also getting hungry. The squirrels and rats were trusting, I realized. Too trusting. I could easily sate myself, quickly, covertly, without causing too much of an upset.

But that's wrong. They breathe, they think, they live as you do.

Yes, but… I'm hungry.

Besides, rodents were small… small and insignificant. They were an inferior species. Yes, inferior species.

Kind of like those trash-diving raccoons, too.

How I Killed the Drama

Before I killed the drama, I had to meet it head on, face-to-face.

And its name was Harold Larkens.

I met him during the brief two years I was a traveling salesman for a medical equipment company that will currently remain nameless. Oh, but that sort of discretion is just old habit now, I'd say. Why should they remain nameless? Because of my fear? Because of my embarrassment at having two years' worth of paychecks signed by crooks?

No, old habit now. The company's name was East Morrison Medical Supply Group. I toted their shit from town to town, doctor to doctor, smiling for them, being proud for them, giving them an amiable mascot face with which their customers could associate them, sprinkling the last drops of my acting talent on hocking stuff that probably hastened the Reaper's hand more than stayed it.

Am I remorseful? Hateful? Vengeful? Guilty?

Nah.

That's because I met Harold Larkens. That's because the universe had the good sense to put our two hotel rooms together that night, back to back, like buddies comparing height.

I was on my way to Chicago for some medical conference I would never make it to, and, because of lagging funds and my recent inability to get a hold of East Morrison for better accommodations, I'd checked into a two-bit roach shack. Chicago was only a fifteen-hour drive from my hometown, and I hate flying. Hated, I should say. So I limited my time in the air as much as possible. But nothing bothers me now.

That's because I met Harry Larkens. That's because, soon after I met Harry Larkens, I killed him.

Hey, he asked me to.

***

The sobbing noise filtered easily through the thin walls of the Orchid Acres Motel. Normally I wouldn't have paid attention, especially with Victoria's many secrets sprawled across my lap (that catalogue was with me the entire two years), but there was something off about this sobbing. Crying usually carried the weight of regret, depression, or mourning, but I couldn't classify this one. It was just… different.

As I listened, I had to laugh: between, and within, every sob, stutter and hiccup were distant burps—often reaching belch status—farts, sharp, twangy "Ha!" kinds of laughs, sneezes, and coughs. And every one of them different from their normal counterparts, the ones you'd encounter on buses and subways and planes. They were so heavy and so authoritarian, as though they took themselves to be the *first* fart, or cough, or sneeze, or belch, and were all perversely proud of it.

Yet the persistent sobbing, that horrible, unearthly sobbing, seemed to destroy any notion of pride.

I'm not sure how long I sat there, drinking in his misery, morbidly entertained by it as it infested my admittedly fragile wellbeing. My erection shot. I started to think too much, and with every sob, hiccup, and gurgle noise, the thinking grew heavier and darker.

If I didn't do something, I concluded, come morning the local police could conceivably have two back-to-back suicides on their hands. So I zipped up, straightened myself, and went next door.

Raising my hand to knock, I saw the door was slightly ajar. Slowly, I stepped into the room, knocking as I went. "Excuse me?"

No immediate reaction. I opened the door further. Nothing appeared out of order except for the man sitting cross-legged on the bed, back arched, head slumped as though he'd suffered a stroke while meditating. What struck me was how pristine everything was—from the crisply made bed to the default position of the remote atop the TV, all appeared untouched. There didn't even seem to be any luggage.

I watched the man's body spasm with tears, listened to the blackly humorous noises that continued emanating from his body.

Maybe he's dying.

"Excuse me?" I said again, this time louder. "Are you all right, sir?"

"I can't stop this," he said, remaining fixed, head still down.

179

"Stop what?"

He looked at me, his eyes swallowing my attention whole. "You'll have to stop this for me."

"What?"

"Yes. You're here. I've tried many others, but they can't do it. My belches get the best of them."

"Why? What did you have for dinner?"

"It's not like that. Step closer and see for yourself."

Cautiously I obeyed, taking two soft strides into the room. Harry farted and I felt a wave of ecstatic juvenile lust rush me, far more potent than with Victoria's luscious secrets. The scent stayed in my nostrils and soon the erotic feelings simmered into domestic adoration. Familial love. Fiftieth anniversary love.

Then Harry belched and I felt a stinking jealousy the likes of which I'd never encountered before.

When Harry sneezed, I felt unprecedented anger. Frustration.

And when he coughed, he coughed up a potent case of fear that, for mere moments, assigned a phobia to everything around me.

He hiccupped, and sadness swept me. A lonely, hollow melancholy I'd never experienced, even in the two years spent isolated on the road.

Yet when that spurt of "Ha!'" laughter fired from his throat, I was a giddy kid again, laughing myself silly sitting in the back of some cheesy matinee my buddies and I just snuck into.

"My organs," Harry said through the tears. "My organs aren't normal."

"I would… uh, I would guess so," I stammered, still mystified by the rapid procession of sensations.

"Instead of lungs I have… well, a set of fears," he said. "I've been told they look like big livers. My love is a sphincter. Actually, it's your love, too. It's everyone's."

Another "Ha!" came out and I laughed, but I'd already been laughing out of puzzled discomfort.

Then I smelled something else. Stepping in closer, I detected wave after wave of a ripe body odor, and I felt a poignant curiosity: a sense of wide-eyed, gawking amazement. Wonder. The permeating inquisitiveness, exploratory restlessness, which often made men insane and society saner.

"It's all in that, that curiosity," Harry said. "The skin contains it all, that begins it and nurtures it all. But now… now…"

He couldn't finish his sentence. There was an unsteady pause.

Then:

"I want you to kill me. Please."

"What?"

"I want you to kill me. To end my life."

"Why?"

"It will bring me great relief. It will bring *all* of you great relief." He lowered his eyes. "I have… I have cancer."

I blinked. "I'm sorry."

"You don't understand," he said. "This cancer will affect you all."

"I can't do that. I can't kill someone." At least not directly, I thought, thinking of East Morrison.

"That's what you all say," Harry said. "You're just smelling my farts and hearing my laughs. But if I set foot outside long enough, you would all change your tune."

"What in blazes are you talking about? What's your name?"

Beneath the darkness of his voice slipped the words, "Harold Larkens."

"Okay, Harold, I'm only here to help you—"

"Right, I realize that. So many people have said they want to help me. They claim they want to, but nobody has actually fulfilled my simple request."

"You mean, killing you?"

He nodded. "My gas gets in the way."

"What do you mean 'if you set foot outside, you would all change your tune?'"

"During daylight. I haven't been in the sun for many years. I'm allergic."

"Allergic. You mean—"

"I sneeze a lot."

My mind quickly replayed the anger I'd felt when he sneezed. I shuddered.

"Photic sneeze reflex," I blurted out, recalling the syndrome from my relatively superficial dip in the medical field.

"Is that what I have?" he said.

"Sounds like it. Some people walk out into the sun and just start sneezing uncontrollably. My brother is like that. He lives in Hawaii, which doesn't make much sense."

Suddenly Harold let loose with a loud "Ha!," and his

expression was one of pleasant surprise. Much of his eyes, however, remained clouded in that unshakable autumn.

"I have an idea," he said.

I backed up a step.

"Sunrise is in five hours," he said. "Will you take me to a secluded area? You'd be closest to me. You'd feel the brunt of it. You might even get all of it. And it would cloud you, drown out every other sensation so you'd have no choice but to destroy me."

"Harold," I said, now in the doorway. "I don't think—"

All at once, he burst from the bed, ruffling the crispness of the sheets, and lunged at me, grabbing both my arms. I was stifled, ensconced in this man's powerful body odor of curiosity and gas of love and empathy. I think what got me most, however, were the hiccups, the diaphragm glitches overwhelming me with hollowness, loneliness so extraordinary and desperate I opted to entertain any company I could get my hands on.

"Please," he said. "I cannot exist any longer. The hiccups came the most frequently. I've been hiccupping for ages. Please."

"Harold…"

"It will all be okay, don't you see?" he said. "It will all be okay afterward. You've got to believe me."

He sneezed suddenly and, in a thoughtless flash, my fist plowed into his cheek. He stumbled back against the door, blood dribbling down his face.

Harold Larkens smiled. "Please," he repeated.

I didn't care much for psychological introspection,

though "introspection" entailed monitoring my thoughts as he confronted me with his words and odors. I had no idea what went on in my head then. I didn't care to analyze.

I opened my bag of supplies, asking if any instrument would prove most efficient for the job. He didn't have a preference, but indicated the scalpel as being the "best we've got now."

He assured me, once again, it wouldn't matter in the end. Nothing would.

I drove him three hours to a high point overlooking Lake Michigan.

***

Like a mother cautiously peeking into her child's room to survey the mess, the sun rose and cast its revealing light upon the land, a massive maternal eye driving the night back into the Earth, to see mankind into a new age.

Harold held out his arms, closed his eyes, and soaked in the warmth.

I loved him, I was jealous of him, I was embarrassed by him, I laughed at him, I feared him, I was all sorts of things to him; I was a fount of emotion.

And the sneezing began.

They came in such rapid succession, negating the occasional chuckle and fart. Boiling frustration became anger, mutated into rage.

"Feel it," Harold said. "Feel it and *drown* in it. Please…"

The heat consumed.

I took the scalpel and stabbed him in the anger. It bled,

spurting every which way in a wild and pathetic assault on the air. Then I cut open his sadness and it dribbled limply down his skin, pooling at his feet and mine. I punched him in the happiness, exploding sunlight from our minds, and then severed his jealousy, mangled his hate, broke his fear, tore out his guilt, and clobbered his laughter and silliness.

And Harold Larkens fell, collapsed before me. The sun grew hotter, brighter.

I stood there for quite a long time, staring at his body.

He was dead.

Hm.

So that's how I killed the drama.

World peace, I guess?

Who cares.

The Mystery Manager

The second my life ended, I met a man called Edgar Murkencap.

Yes, a strange surname, but one whose first four letters I soon deemed quite appropriate given his job title at this… well, this level of existence.

It took me a moment to adjust to this place, this bland work station where Edgar sat at a lone cubicle in a swivel chair. It was an afterlife, sure, but not the one I'd been expecting, having nothing to do with paradise or damnation. Though given my lifetime dedication to my faith I wasn't particularly expecting the latter.

"Who are you?" I asked.

He swiveled around to meet my gaze.

"Greetings! Name's Edgar Murkencap. I do Mystery Management on your planet. I make sure that that inquisitive passion, that urge to explore, remains strong among your species. Without it, your very thirst for life might dry up! We can't have that, can we?"

"I don't think I understand," I said. "You keep things hidden from us?"

"In a sense. I'm the one who keeps away all empirical evidence of Bigfoot, the one who blinks away planes and ships in the Bermuda Triangle, blurs the photographs of the Chupacabra or the Loch Ness Monster. Whenever I see a legend growing in your cultures, I maintain it as a gardener might a flower, watering the hope, blooming the faith. But I always keep them just beyond reach."

"Why?"

"To keep your souls hungry, of course! But now that you've left this first stage of existence, I can feed yours… before you move on."

"All I want to know," I said, "is God."

"That's not really my area," said Edgar.

"Huh?"

"Sure, I manage *your* world's mysteries," he said. "But some things have to remain a mystery here. Otherwise…" Edgar Murkencap swiveled back to his station. "What would keep *me* going?"

The Principle

Let's lay the groundwork here. My twin brother Charles and I are known as the relayers. The big boss man, constantly looming behind us, is the reporter. In fact, he does more than report. He runs everything around, above and below us. My brother and I have a very close relationship with him. He sponsors us, even though our services drain a good deal of his resources. Yet, make no mistake about it: we are essential agents to the operation.

Our time, however, is short.

The big boss man keeps us both on short, optic leashes, snug in our home sockets. Despite the proximity in which we work, he refuses to accept, much less report, half the things we relay to him. Shadows twisting in the broken places and ragged slits of the world. Space bleeding internally, issuing corrupted dark matter—a kind of amorphous, shifting, flowing sludge all around us. Although everyone technically sees it all, it is seldom reported. Charles and I don't even know what this dark sludge really is, but we've seen it pour into this dimension, trickle across the ages, a growing cancer on time, rotting and destroying.

We've seen it shift and fit snugly into the heart of a

passing woman, or the colon of a middle-aged man, or the bone marrow of a young child. We've seen it cover the entirety of two massive skyscrapers moments before they were reduced to fire and rubble. It covers cars, trains, animals and people. It trips them or makes them sneeze or sends them plummeting to their death.

It grows monsters, too.

Some of them are truly bestial, although Charles and I have never seen one taller than around ten or eleven feet. They stride through dimensions unseen, crawling from the tar-black sea that washes its ghastly tide upon the soul, as we no doubt evolved from our own sea. I doubt any of them possess the faintest glimmer of intelligence—they just feed, that's all they do. They eat everything. They take gardens and buildings and homes as appetizers, dine on sentient beings for the main course, and pick their teeth with the fragile constructs of this reality.

None of this—the black substance, the beasts, the frenzied feeding and decay—ever "came," and by came I mean arrived. Nor do they have a beginning. They are the Principle.

They are the one rule.

Our boss doesn't want to acknowledge this. He chooses to discard over half of what we tell him, not realizing the danger posed by such a choice. Not realizing that denial will ultimately impede survival, even though ironically, "survival" is the boss's evolutionary excuse for not processing our information.

Some reporters, however, have accepted the sights of the

Principle, with mixed results. Granted, many who are given a naked viewing cannot bear it. Often, the sludge—that horrible, shadowy sludge, whatever it is—ensconces them in its world, the world before the universe began, holding them not in darkness or light, but in a kind of chaos. More often than not, they are thusly carried to the morgue or, if the reporter still manages minimal functionality, sealed away from civilization.

That word is bitterly amusing—civilization. Many might reconsider its definition knowing what waits just behind it, only a centimeter of perception away.

But there are a few who acclimate to it all, who see the creatures as they are and accept them and thrive with full working senses within the Principle. It is to this wakened state that we must communally aspire. Their predation depends on ignorance, too much of which is willed by reporters.

Tragically, had our boss understood this, we might've saved Charles. For some time now he has been infested with that dark shifting clay, his relaying abilities compromised. He manages to make do, though, and the boss has kept him functional throughout. Doubtless he will soon be done with, leaving me alone to bear this burden.

Charles won't be coming back—either he'll be replaced with a glass replica, or superficially covered.

Nothing lasts. I fear even I might not be around much longer. The sludge that infected Charles... some of it remains, and grows still.

On the boss.

And on me.

Skeptic

"You don't believe me."

"Not that I don't believe you, really. More that I think it was just a faulty experience. A clearer knowing. A dream. A feverish delusion, perhaps."

"I don't know. It was something much more than that. I could... I don't know how to describe it."

"So I take it I'm in for another sermon."

"What makes you say that?"

"Trust me, I can tell. And now that you've had this experience—"

"It was my experience, not yours."

"Okay..."

"So trying to convince you would just be in vain."

"It's about time you finally realized that."

"I don't understand why you're so unwilling to even consider the possibility of experiencing and feeling the—"

"Geez, here we go again. Do you realize how astronomically— beyond astronomically, even—impossible what you're suggesting would be? Do you even realize how improbable it would be for matter to get to a life-containing state? I mean, even if it did, imagine how awfully *restricting* that would be.

Why would we want to do it in the first place? And where would all that energy be stored? How low would we have to go, vibrationally?"

"I can only tell you my experience. I can't answer all those questions. I don't think we were ever meant to."

"Well as long as you keep talking about this, I'm going to keep asking these questions."

"You can't accept something on faith. I've known that about you."

"There can't be anything to accept. And listen—I've heard stories like yours before and they don't sound like anything I'd want."

"You don't want experience? You only want to think? To wonder?"

"If experience exists, I see it as more of a mixed blessing."

"It's all a blessing!"

"So let me ask you—why did you come back so quickly? Don't those who've claimed to be 'material' say they experienced a lot more than you?"

"It was a taste, is all. I touched the other side. Who knows why I was brought back. It was probably for others."

"Others."

"Yeah. My short time there was for the others that were already there."

"That makes no sense to me."

"It doesn't make much sense to me either. I'm just theorizing."

"Do you mean it was for their benefit?"

"Again, I have no idea."

"This is nonsense."

"I don't know. I just don't know. You don't know. You can only… experience it."

"Oh, I know. I know it's a delusion."

***

"Are you sure you're okay?" he asked, as he handed her the juice.

With a trembling hand she held the glass, rattling the ice, and took a long slow sip, remaining still on the edge of the couch.

"It's perfectly normal to feel upset," he told her. "No one said it would be easy."

The clock ticked in the kitchen. She took a breath and looked at her knees, clutching the quarter-empty glass in her right hand.

"Remember what they said—it's even okay to feel a little, well, disgusted with yourself. But you have to realize why you did this in the first place. You have to think about yourself. You weren't ready. Neither of you were ready."

"Do you think he'll go someplace else?" she said.

"Excuse me?"

"Do you think he'll go someplace else?"

He made a face, hoping it wasn't too condescending.

"He?"

"It was a he. I know it. Or, knew it. I could tell."

"I understand."

"No, you don't. You don't understand. Don't give me that bullshit."

For a moment there was quiet.

"Who knows if he'll go someplace else," he said. "Maybe he will be given to someone else."

"Someone who wants him."

"Right."

She looked at him. "You think I'm deluded, don't you?"

He shrugged. "Not at all."

"It's okay," she said, sipping her drink. "It's okay."

The Hand of Spudd

A rock, that's all it was. A single, lonesome rock.

Or so the Instructor thought as the greasy face and hopeful eyes of Marvin Spudd hovered before him. The boy held out his science project, cupping it with two quivering hands. Under normal circumstances, the Instructor would wonder why such a bright, assiduous student would be so nervous, but with the annual Cosmic Science Fair looming, things nowadays were far from normal. The event cast a large shadow over the following weeks and beckoned every student with its ultimate prize: the immortalization of one's project in a Microverse solar system. Many of the Instructor's students had won before (a lot of them crafting nebulas, black holes, and a wide variety of stars), and for this he was especially noted when all heads turned to the judging panels. Marvin Spudd— or, as all the star and gas-planet builders called him, "Spudd the Dud"—had been laboring away at his planet for nearly a million years, and with each monthly evaluation he'd be told the same thing about the same rock.

"I don't know what you're doin' trying to create a

terrestrial planet," the Instructor said, reclining in his leather throne that overlooked the entire class. Everyone was peering up at Marvin, spitting giggles into their hands, suppressing inevitable mockery. The boy certainly was tenacious, the Instructor had to give him that, but there was a fine line between obsession and tenacity, and Marvin Spudd was now inches from crossing it.

"I dunno, sir, I think I can do it," he answered. His teenage voice crackled like an aluminum can. "Everyone always just builds stuff outta fire and gas, gas 'n fire... I thought it'd be time to do something—"

"Different?" the Instructor finished for him. He leaned forward authoritatively. The students whipped their heads forward, knowing he meant business. "Different..." he repeated, trying to chase Marvin's thoughts. "I commend you, Mr. Spudd, for your perseverance, but I'm afraid I'm just going to tell you what I've told you for the past few thousand years: do something simpler."

He paused, suddenly overcome with a desire to be encouraging. "There's no doubt that you have talent. The fact that you created the skeleton of a terrestrial planet is amazing enough, but it seems that's all you can do, that's your limit. I'd love to see you author, say, a supernova or a gas-monster like Jupiter's project last year." He looked over at Jupiter, a hulking athlete who sat smug and content in his chair. Since receiving first prize at the Cosmic Science Fair, the jock had claimed the popularity crown and now felt the need to make life miserable for everyone else, quite notably young Marvin.

The young man's gaze slowly unhinged. His head rolled downward in embarrassment.

"Remember, son," the Instructor said, trying to make eye contact with him again. "Don't make a universe if you can't first make a galaxy." The Instructor smiled. It was a last-minute attempt to cheer up the boy who had never seen a friend (much less one of the female persuasion), and would surely live with his parents for another few centuries. The attempt, however, was futile, and Marvin glumly returned to his seat. He kept his head low as he entered the spread of classmates before him. He made furtive glances back and forth behind his steel-rimmed glasses, the glasses that acted as telescopes from his seat two light years from the chalkboard.

***

His hands had stopped quivering. There was no need for tension anymore; inherent failures had nothing to worry about.

"Spudd the Dud," somebody rasped in a throaty voice. A flaming comet struck Marvin's right temple. He didn't even bother to look to see who it was, knowing by the snickers that it was Jupiter. He also knew that, before the day was over, an ever bigger spit-comet would undoubtedly be hurtling towards his head. And under those elusive normal circumstances, Marvin Spudd would tell the Instructor, thus landing himself a vicious beating, but today he didn't seem to care. Something told him he'd see Jupiter's row of embattled knuckles scream towards his face one way or the other.

He slumped into his seat and looked at his failed project, scouring and churning it like a child making a wish with a magic eight-ball. Its surface was rugged ("You could *cut* yourself on that thing, boy!" his father had said), with a spherical array of craters, spewing volcanoes, and a core that bubbled with scalding flame.

The bell clanged, ending class. For Marvin Spudd, it was also the end of a long period of arduous labor. Throughout the entire time, he'd no doubt inured somewhat to the degrading and often mind-numbing task of crafting a planet, but today had been the final blow.

If I was to ever get it right, it woulda happened by now, he thought, swallowing hard the realization.

Woulda happened by now.

He walked home along an uneventful path that day, his project nestled somewhere between two textbooks and a half-eaten lunch in his backpack. That night, he tossed it in the trash and spit on it in disgust.

Day Four

"Marvin, get up! You're late for school!"

He blinked twice, feeling the thin layer of sleep that'd collected in his eyes. Normally he'd drag himself from the comfy warmth of his sheets with zombie-like lethargy. But today he felt rejuvenated, well-rested, the kind of feeling he got waking up at noon on weekends and knowing there was no Instructor, no work, no jock's fist, and no sneering cheerleaders to look forward to. He'd accepted his defeat and now felt a sense of calm and uneasy security that he hadn't felt in quite a long while. As his uncle had once said, "Losers are the real winners." At the time, Marvin had attributed the phrase to the man's waning mental state, but today he figured there couldn't have been a more appropriate saying to sum up everything that now clutched at his own thoughts.

"Oh, and sweetie, please take out your trash before you leave. It's full."

Marvin tossed on a shirt conveniently lying on the floor then picked up the trashcan. It foamed with crumpled papers and artwork. He took it through the house, made his way outside and began dumping the contents into the black canister that sat alone in the alleyway behind his house.

As the garbage rained down into the canister's square maw, he noticed something: a luminescent sphere of blue and green, approximately the same size as—

Wait a minute.

Was that his project? *His* project? The one he'd spat on in contempt and left for dead?

He reached down and pulled it out, analyzing it with emotions that ranged from fear to confusion to a weird, sunny feeling of love. Most of the planet's surface was blanketed with water, presumably from Marvin's saliva, except for a small rocky outpost that had abandoned its crater-ridden mug and gotten a lush green facelift. Stupefied with amazement, he rushed back in and placed the project carefully on his desk, directly under the glistening eye of his desk lamp. The waters swirled and flowed methodically, touching shores with a salty caress.

"Marvin, let's go! The bus will be here any minute!"

Without hesitation he bolted from the room, locking the door behind him and sealing the growing secret within his own four walls.

Day Five

The next day saw even more growth. During the time he'd been at school, the planet had spawned tiny little organisms that avidly ate one another and lumbered across the landscape like the scaly tyrants they were. The numerous regions of the planet (or, the sections of rock that hadn't been hit with Marvin's saliva) were splitting apart and drifting away to form their own positions on the sphere. A lot of this had happened while he was sitting bored in the classroom, and he kicked himself for having missed it.

Tomorrow, he thought proudly, on the verge of saying it out loud. Tomorrow I will stay here all day and watch 'em. He had to document everything that occurred with this new project of his, otherwise it'd be scoffed out of the Fair like all his other failed attempts. No doubt the evolution of a minuscule form of life was groundbreaking, but Marvin wanted to make sure he knew why they'd evolved—he wanted to have the upper hand on anyone who thought coughing up swirling balls of gases was some impressive achievement.

Not too much later, he would accidentally spill soda on it, dispatching a swarm of acid unto the planet and destroying nearly every creature on the land and in the water. As Marvin beat his head against the wall, thinking he'd taken yet another academic K.O., a new kind of animal began to emerge from the charred mountains and seas not minutes thereafter.

Day Six

Marvin stayed up all night, trampling the red-eye hours with an endless marathon of caffeine and raw fascination. The creatures that had developed the night before (just before midnight, actually, and Marvin knew this because his favorite TV show had just ended) were reproducing like mad and evolving at lightning speed.

At one point, he had to turn down the air conditioning in his room, since its frigid breath had given the planet a thick coat of ice, but the period only lasted half a minute and the new creatures survived with flying colors. As their society developed, so did their minds—and as their minds developed, so did their consciousness. They built weapons, kept warm by rubbing sticks and creating sparks with stones, drew diagrams and looked skyward almost longingly.

As before, there were plenty of other life forms populating the planet, but none held Marvin's interest quite as much as these new ones did. They grew as tiny versions of himself—or any other entity in the Macroverse, for that matter—and began revering him in numerous forms that he found either insulting or flattering. The awe-inspiring realization came to him not much longer after he first caught wind of this mental connection with these beings, and it struck him with a blow that hit harder and sank deeper than any jock's fist could ever dream.

To his eerie fascination, Marvin began to notice something as the creatures grew: they could sense his presence. They were aware.

"Marvin?" came a familiarly shrill voice just beyond the door. It was his mother. The jolt brought him out of his glassy-eyed trance. He glanced towards the doorway, and when the knob began to shake with his mother's suspicions, he was glad he'd remembered to lock it.

"What, Mom? What is it?" He marveled at the mountain his voice seemed to scale in that split second. It began low, almost like his father's, rose to that of a woman's, then finally dipped back down again like an oar into the ripples of the sea.

"You have to get ready for school, what's going on in there?"

Thinking quickly, he conjured some phlegm and coughed twice. "I don't think I'd better go today, Mom, I'm not feeling too well. Something's probably going around school." He wrapped a blanket around himself and unlocked the door. His mother poked her head in, and for a moment he was afraid she might be able to sense the rush of frenzied activity that'd just taken place. Ants crawled on his skin as she analyzed him curiously.

"You look a little flushed," she said, feeling his forehead. "Very well then, stay home, but stay in bed, got it? I don't want to come home and find you running around playing with your models or raiding the fridge."

Marvin sat down on his bed, splattering wrinkles across his blanket. With a sudden pang of horror he realized he'd neglected to cover up his science project, which sat idly on his desk, harboring quite possibly the most amazing secret of all time, a secret so enigmatic that even Marvin was kept out of the loop. He couldn't wait to share it with the world. He could just see the look on Jupiter's face when the ribbon bypassed his planet and landed squarely on Marvin's. But, first things first. He needed to be able to explain what had happened, needed to uncover and articulate this newfound recipe for life.

As Marvin sat on his bed that day, pretending to be ill, conflicting thoughts waged war in his head. On one hand, he would probably knock his mother's socks off with this discovery, no doubt securing her endless love and affection for another thousand years and putting to rest all those "Why can't you be more like so-and-so" spiels. However, he also felt he needed to be close with these creatures, to be the only higher force in their midst so as not to bombard their minds and hinder any evolutionary progress. How would they react knowing this "God" of theirs was nothing but a high school nerd whose only previous moment of glory was second place in the elementary school physics bee?

"Hope you feel better soon, sweetie-pie," his mother cried, already halfway down the hall.

"I told you to stop calling me that, Mom."

The slam of the front door was his only answer—and his ticket to freedom.

Throwing off the blanket, he immediately resumed his position under the pyramid of light cast by his desk lamp. There he watched with glazed fascination as the creatures shot up the ladder of knowledge and technology with the fervor of a prison escapee. Within the minutes since Marvin had talked to his mother, they'd constructed behemoth triangular structures in the desert, had engulfed an impressive amount of land and were now beginning to formulate mass perceptions of their "God" and who, or what, he actually was. Marvin was ecstatic, and through his own happiness he found that the emotion was also bred on the surface of his planet. Somehow, in the last few minutes, the growing collective consciousness of these beings had staked out real estate in his own head. He could feel them, inside and out.

Not much later, Marvin was amazed to see them mimicking his thoughts, mimicking the world of the Macroverse with their laws, schooling, and general ways of life. It was as though they could unconsciously read the files of his own view of the Macroverse, using this connection as a birth canal to construct a civilization in a matter of short minutes. As their minds developed and were polished in the speeding minutes Marvin became more and more aware of the bond he held with these creatures—these creatures who had apparently arisen from a glob of spit and nothing more. It was all too fast for Marvin, and he began to have doubts about showing this wonder off to anyone else, at least for now. If he was having trouble wrapping his head around this, how would the Instructor or judges or others like Jupiter react? They'd declare it a fraud, a typical method of dealing with (or rather, not having to deal with) the unexplained mysteries of the Cosmos.

Marvin's bladder began to swell achingly with nature's usual morning call. He headed quickly for the bathroom, was gone for only a few seconds, and by the time he returned to his desk the creatures had erected sprawling cities, governments, highly-advanced technology that shattered barriers and uncovered new quirks about the planet's nature (with some things that Marvin hadn't even known about). Their imagination continued to grow and thrive on this new breadth of knowledge—they'd even educated themselves on the entire history of Marvin's planet, which they dubbed "Earth"—but something was withering, and quite noticeably at that. Surprisingly, he discovered what a difference a bathroom break could make: in that ephemeral skip of time, the connection he'd shared with them had been fractured, thus leaving the now science-based creatures to wonder whether or not he really existed.

I'm here, guys, he thought, feeling an odd rush of panic. I'm here, don't worry, I'm always here…

Discoveries of all shapes and sizes came and went in milliseconds, often without Marvin even knowing it. They seemed to like to kill one another in mass quantities, and this desire was only enflamed by their progressing society. In a starkly confusing conundrum, Marvin began to see them as wanting to learn more about life in order to cause death.

The bond of consciousness between the beings and their creator (or, originator, rather) was still strong, and it served as a double-seedling for impregnating both minds. At the same time the creatures continued to spread, create, and destroy in a seemingly obsessive-compulsive manner. Marvin was being fed an overwhelming barrage of emotional data.

Scattered remnants of love, fear, envy, and a flood of other emotions attacked his thoughts and shook a sleeping insanity. But through it all was one consistent emotion, one overarching sensation woven too deep in the creatures' innate fabric to ever ignore. It was what fueled much of their advancement in technology, and was now the one thing that had him doubting his choice of keeping this "Earth" a secret.

It was hatred, coupled with the mind-boggling indifference to nature. Marvin's nature.

It was around then that the explosions began.

With a terrible dawning thought, he realized fate was playing a cruel joke on him. In his room he held a piece of the Unknown, a magic trick from an unseen magician, spawned purely from the chemicals and energy of the Macroverse. Marvin Spudd held the secret of life in his palms that day, and as he frantically burst from the house, cupping his precious stupid rock the same way he had on the day of the last evaluation, he knew that the secret of life was relegated to, and only to, the wand of that unknown magician.

One by one the explosions scarred the planet, and Marvin could feel the radioactive heat swallow his entire forearms. The project reeked with the noisome stench of decay, and in those moments all sorts of thoughts threaded their way through Marvin's head, so chaotic and jumbled that they wove a painful knot in the center of his mind.

As the dwindling stem of their connection dissipated and fell away with the final explosion, Marvin began to cry.

He fell to his knees, only one block from Macroverse High, where surely everyone else was being commended on their standard run-of-the-mill supernovas and asteroid belts and all the other meaningless components of the Microverse that swept the Cosmic Fair every million years.

"They were just as meaningless," he sighed, his head lowered much in the same way the creatures had done in worshipping him.

With a heavy chest and a pounding heart, he turned and walked back towards home.

***

He stood over the toilet, palming his jagged, barren project like so many of Macroverse High's athletes did with their footballs or basketballs. The lid was open, and he hesitated.

Marvin peered closely at the charred remains, his heart feeling as though it had a dumbbell hanging from it. The heaviness in his chest was nearly unbearable now, and he knew he had to rid himself of this thing once and for all. Like a wheel, it'd cycled back to its original state – lifeless and barren and devoid of any sort of features that would land it the Blue Ribbon at the Fair, much less the esteemed Macroversal Prize for Science.

Tragically, Marvin Spudd had had no idea how those little particles of consciousness had grown—was it simply the arbitrary combination of his spit with the surrounding air molecules? Or was it something less tangible and more spiritual in nature, a single dream, wafting through the unconscious mind of its Macroverse agent and materializing in ways better left unexplained? Whatever it was, it'd helped to lift Marvin, at least temporarily, from a seemingly endless void, a void where he was and would always be Spudd the Dud, the lanky pole of pimples. Unwittingly, those creatures had done more for him in an hour than any other entity in this entire Cosmos. They knew he was there, at least for the most part, and knew he'd somehow created them. In the latter seconds of their civilization, they'd taken on the role of life-giver themselves and, ironically, came closer to the ultimate secret than Marvin or any other higher form had. Yet they knew not how to wield the power of their own pseudo-Godliness, and that was their ultimate downfall.

In one fluid motion, Marvin Spudd tossed the project into the small triangular pool of water and shut the lid. He couldn't watch, and by the time the gurgles and belches of the flushing toilet had ceased, only small traces of burnt residue remained. He wondered which one of the Microverse sewers would receive the broken treasure, then wondered why he even bothered to care. It'd be dumped somewhere, far off, away from Marvin's attention and possibly prone to another rotation of life's wheel.

Would all that happen again? He didn't think so, and even if it should, the timeframe was so utterly fleeting that he now felt privileged to be the only entity to ever have witnessed the rise and fall of such creatures. Who knows how many other planets might have spawned and destroyed organisms in the wink of an eye? Not even a Macroverse entity's supposed omnipotence would be sufficient—or quick enough—to catch that.

The pebble-sized remnants of the planet now floated aimlessly, adrift like one of its former species, a jellyfish, with no place to go, but knowing they should keep moving.

Marvin would later think the same thing about the lives he'd once created, all of whom were now nothing more than shadows in his memory.

The next day, the end of the week, brought rest.

The Haddelton Gelatin

One of the small blemishes on the Pennsylvania countryside, Haddelton was a place that, barring a visit from a presidential candidate, would hardly attract much attention. Stories had begun to spread, however, of a certain delicacy exclusive to the town—an unexpected treat for the taste buds allegedly not sold but offered for free to anyone willing to seek out and darken the door of the small, unassuming house of a Gilbert and Edna Frankfurt.

Their jell-o is just insane, one online poster had written. *Just freakin out of this world.*

Gelatin, corrected another. *Jell-o is a brand, and an insult to the Haddelton stuff, which is, yes, pretty damn amazing.*

Freelance columnist Steven Fries, a stocky fellow of almost forty years, had made Haddelton his destination, his X on his map. After a staff job at the *Baltimore Sun*, his writing hand had broken loose and for five years he'd been writing articles for various publications across the country. In doing so Fries had carved his own very identifiable niche, offering quirky and informative columns that were, as many saw them, refreshing breaks from the plethora of murder and political scandal and celebrity gossip stinking up so many papers and magazines.

Part of his motivation had been the unsuccessful attempt to locate any previous articles written on the Haddelton gelatin. Sure, there were many message board postings, and some quick blurb here and there about its "tasty and sugary divinity" (his personal favorite line), but no real report or interview that dug further than the taste buds. The word rode solely on the mouths of those who'd experienced it for themselves.

He had the address, so asking a clerk or gas station attendant wasn't necessary. He was glad of it. Fries sensed eyes on him as he drove through town, and they didn't feel particularly friendly. Many of the people he saw were on both ends of the age spectrum, either old or young, and he wondered with cynicism if Haddelton believed in schools or nursing homes.

The Frankfurt house was just as he'd expected it —a one-story house standing on weeds, with a lawn no gardener would touch if he enjoyed his sanity. Foliage was spattered around it with the disarray of soap suds on the shower floor.

Old fogeys, he thought. As they deteriorate, so does everything around them.

Fries knocked three times. Inside he heard voices and a shuffling sound. Soon a woman of about seventy answered. She was exactly what Fries had envisioned: petite frame, wrinkled skin, and a dandelion poof of wispy hair atop her head.

"Yes?" she said.

"Hello, are you Mrs. Edna Frankfurt?"

"I am." She smiled, but it was only in her lips—her eyes

remained untouched, appearing indifferent and, Fries thought, a bit sad. "I presume you'd like to try it?"

"Try… the gelatin?"

She nodded.

"Yes, I would, thank you."

She gestured him in. Gilbert Frankfurt was in the kitchen, fiddling and clambering about with pots and dishes. When he called out to ask who it was, Mrs. Frankfurt told him it was a young man, stopping short of his name as she allowed Fries to fill in the blank.

"My name is Steven Fries," he said. "I'm a freelance columnist. I've been hearing some things about your homemade gelatin. Thought I'd see it for myself."

Edna indicated the kitchen table, an atlas of rust. "Won't you sit down?"

He sat in the chair. It groaned under his weight.

"Did we filet the latest batch?" Edna asked her husband.

"Yes, we did. I did."

Filet?

"So how long have you two lived here?" Fries asked.

"About ten years now," Gil Frankfurt said over running water. He slung a rag over his shoulder and turned towards his wife. "It is coming up on ten years, isn't it?"

"Yes, dear, ten years this December."

"So you really haven't been here too long," Fries said, restraining himself from adding, "for people your age."

"Not if you count some of our friends, no. We have a neighbor, Bert Stiles. He's been in his place for over forty-five years. He's outlasted three wives, and even one of his sons."

"Wow," Fries said. His gaze shot straight to the bowl of gelatin that Edna was now bringing him. Although he hadn't expected the commercial kind, Fries was startled by how exotic, how foreign, the stuff looked.

"Here you go," Edna said, placing the dish before him. "I should warn you that it goes through some folks pretty fast. It's mostly water, after all. I mean, we think it is."

Fries nodded, not really listening, and analyzed the wobbling lump not a foot below his chin. The gelatin was every shade of blue imaginable. Some areas he even perceived to be black. The substance quivered, suffering chills and tremors as, like an alien spacecraft, Fries' spoon descended upon its glistening cumulus surface.

Not really tasty to the eyes.

All superficial judgments fell away once the taste melted on his tongue and swirled around his mouth. His favorite quote of "tasty and sugary divinity" reached new meaning, no longer just a hyperbolic quip.

"Enjoying it, Mr. Fries?" Edna asked.

"Very much so. I never thought gelatin, of all things, could be this good. How on earth do you do this?"

"You may soon find out."

"Has no one been told the secret?" he said. "I've never read anything but praise. I understand if you don't want to tell me, but—"

"Many of your type have come around asking about it, wanting to publish it in their books or papers or whatnot, but we couldn't give them anything. They couldn't help us, so we couldn't help them."

He had no idea what to make of that statement, but at the moment, during the little orgasms in his taste buds, Fries didn't particularly care. The stuff was outstanding. Then suddenly it hit him. They hadn't been kidding—not more than three minutes after finishing the bowl an immense pressure swelled in his bladder. He excused himself from the table, rushed to the bathroom and relieved himself. For the duration of the stream Fries didn't notice anything, only rolled his head from side to side, his eyes half-closed in the bliss of release.

Zipping up, he noticed his urine. It was blue.

Explanations darted furiously through his head, from toilet bowl cleaner to the effect of light through the bathroom window. The gelatin he'd just eaten didn't escape suspicion, either—after all, asparagus did its own noisome trick on bladder contents. Why couldn't that gelatin have done something to the color?

It didn't look natural.

A knock on the door.

"Mr. Fries?"

Gil Frankfurt.

"Yes?"

"May I ask you not to flush the toilet, please?" he asked kindly. "Something's screwy with our plumbing. We're having someone come first thing tomorrow to fix it. I'm sorry I didn't mention it earlier."

"Um, sure." Fries put the lid down, not wanting to look at his blue urine that he wished to God he could just flush away right then and there. But ruining these folks' entire plumbing system wasn't exactly something he wanted to risk.

"Thank you."

When he came out into the living room, Gil Frankfurt was washing his bowl and spoon. Edna sat at the kitchen table, arms folded delicately, gazing at Fries with strained compassion.

"It looks as though we can tell you," she said, getting up.

"Oh really?" he said.

Drying the dishes, Gil said, "Follow Edna into the backyard. I'll be out in a moment."

Through a ragged screen door hanging from only one hinge, Fries went with the old woman to the backyard, the lawn of which was just as weedy and patchy as the one out front.

Gil followed Fries out the door. They convened around a section of grass. Near the center of the lawn was a large, round discoloration. Fries found that, if he looked right at it, the spot blended with the rest of the lawn, coming into focus only through squinting or out of the corner of his eye. He bent down and pulled up a clump of the affected grass, sifting through individual blades in his palm. They were tinted blue.

"This is where it lands, every month," Gil said.

"What do you mean?" Fries asked.

"The gelatin," Gil said. "It comes around the thirteenth or fourteenth of every month. Just plops straight out of the sky. Sometimes it has stuff in it: rocks, little meteors. A few times we've found animals and plants in there, and once in a while they're alive."

Filet.

He shuddered. "You're serious."

"Of course I am. Why do you think we don't advertise this stuff to anyone? Why do you think we don't normally tell people like you how Haddelton gelatin is made? No one would really believe us, and no one would want to believe us. But everyone loves it."

"So this stuff literally just falls from the sky?" Fries said.

They nodded.

"And lands in the same place, at the same time, every month?"

Nodded again.

"It's been happening for some time, apparently, even before we moved in. I suppose the previous owners got fed up with it, or were just too unnerved to keep living here. But we love it. It makes for a great snack, and at our age we welcome the chance to entertain."

"How do you even know this stuff is real gelatin then?" Fries said. "How do you know it's not, like... space-trash?"

"It's not real gelatin, actually. Normal gelatin doesn't taste that good, plain and simple."

"What the hell *is* it then?"

"Günter tells us it's spacetime."

"Spacetime?" Fries said.

"That's what we've been told, anyway."

"Wait. Who is Günter?"

"Oh, he's an alien repairing the space-time, or at least he's trying to. Nice young man. We were watching *Wheel of Fortune* at the time, so not much of his explanation got through, but you know about the hole in the ozone layer?"

"Um, yeah…"

"Well, apparently the same sort of deal is happening further up, in space. There's a big hole in space-time, and chunks fall off and become crumbling debris. Unfortunately, it appears some of the debris falls into our backyard, but as we just said. and as you can clearly see, we take advantage of it."

"You've… had contact with extraterrestrial intelligence?"

"What does that mean? I'm afraid we don't—"

"Aliens, it means you've talked to aliens. Real aliens."

"Well, yes, that's what Günter said he was."

"And his name is Günter and you were watching *Wheel of Fortune* at the time?"

Again they nodded, in tandem. Fries had nothing to say to that. He couldn't respond, as the English language he knew offered nothing for a reaction to such a thing.

"Why me?" he asked. "Why are you telling me this?"

"Most reporters, or investigators, people of your kind," Gil began, "don't try the gelatin for themselves. Yet, they want to know all the secrets behind its creation and its popularity. I don't particularly understand it—maybe they just don't like the look of it when they actually see it."

"It did look a bit, well, off-putting," Fries added, not making eye contact with them.

"I see. Well, in any case, we couldn't be of any help to them. But since you, Mr. Fries, have tried it, we are glad to open our vaults to you."

"Thank you… I guess."

"Now, Günter should be picking you up shortly."

"What?"

"Well, sure. You can't repair something without the material, can you? He'll be able to use what you've eaten to patch up more of that hole he's working on. And according to him, human minds make for some solid roofing. We're the bricks. Space-time is the cement."

"No," Fries sputtered. "No, no, please tell me you're—"

"'Fraid so, buckaroo," Edna said. "But don't worry, no one will really know you're gone. Your life, your memories, everything and everyone you've met in your three or four decades are now sitting in our toilet. You were cleansed. Quite literally you just whizzed away your life not ten minutes ago."

"What?"

"Günter likes to use clean minds. What good is it if the cement is all dirtied up with junk that might get in the way of its job?"

Fries said nothing. He swung glances at the door, wondering what the Frankfurts would do if he were to just bolt through the house and out into the street and away forever from their gelatinous little asylum. His muscles wanted to, as did his brain, but something grounded him. Something was waiting for him on the other side, and he couldn't be sure what. Was it the rest of the town, with their eyes, old and young, sending ghost-glares from nowhere , everywhere? Was it Günter? Was Günter the town? Was Haddelton some haven for delusional folks that liked to lure out-of-towners into their hut of sugary and tasty divinities, only to prey on them? A town of witches to his Hansel, his Gretel?

As the distant whine of a large machine loomed closer, Fries realized no, there was no other explanation. Günter was an alien, a cosmic carpenter, perhaps, and Steven Fries another shingle.

Symbols of Atlantis

In a city so large, diced into many electric, historic, and iconic sections, it's understandable why I was surprised to see the headline about a young whale loitering in the marina. Certainly I'm not complaining about the change in tone or topic: give me a special interest animal story over a carjacking or Hollywood scandal any day. But it was a stray whale, hanging in the murky waters not a hundred feet from Maria's Margarita Bar. Sure, it was fun, but unless it'd come for happy hour, how much more news was there to report? I suppose, though, I shouldn't underestimate the media's ability to milk something. God knows I've done that plenty of times.

When bereft of any real recent inspiration, I usually seek out the quirky stories, the odd anecdotes, to help stir my sometimes narcoleptic muse. This one found me (being on the front page, it probably found almost everyone), and it was something local I could physically experience—a ten-minute drive at most from my home in west Los Angeles, twenty or so minutes from my office on campus. Your guess is as good as mine in terms of what I thought I'd get out of it. Surely there's a primal, Melvillian fascination there.

Before leaving campus for the day, I called my wife, Suzie. The tone of her initial greeting was enough to kindle guilt that I was about to take some time for myself, even if it was a short detour.

"Where are you going?" she asked.

"Down to the marina. I wanted to see that whale they're talking about. Just for a little while. Before it gets dark."

She laughed, but it was a helpless, one-note snap of emotion.

"You won't be long?" she said.

"No." I hesitated. "How's Aaron?"

She sighed. "He had another bad day. His teacher is now suggesting we consider the community day school for the fall."

Hot embers danced in my chest. "Okay. I won't be long. I promise."

I arrived at the marina an hour before sunset. Clots of people stood at the edge of the boardwalk along the wharf, leaning over the rusted railing as I imagined they'd been all day, to catch sight of the creature if it was still there. Since the whale had shown up a day and a half ago, there'd been talk of possibly helping it find its way.

"They say it's a juvenile humpback," I heard one woman remark. "They apparently migrate from Hawaii to Alaska and back every year, and this one might've gotten lost."

We kept watch of the harbor, waiting. The laps and chops of the sun-sparkled water put me in a momentary daze. I noticed I wasn't the only solitary spectator. Several yards down the walk stood an older man, ashen-bearded, his eyes tired, watery—much like mine at the moment. He wore a bulky jacket that had a creased, unclean look to it, and held under his right arm a notebook with a pen clipped to the cover. We made eye contact, but it was fleeting.

Suddenly, there were gasps of delight, and people pointing across the way at the dark, barnacled island rising from the water. The blowholes dilated, releasing misty breath to the evening air, taking with it all thoughts of the last few moments.

***

"Mr. Witky?" said the woman. Her red hair was frayed, her expression tentative, ready to change at a moment's notice. She looked about fifteen years my senior, though her eyes still carried a playful, bohemian glow.

I put down my coffee and stood to shake her hand. "Call me Richard. Or Rich, actually." Having always preferred a first-name basis even with students, I almost quipped how especially old it would make me feel if someone her age addressed me as "Dr. Witky," but thankfully my mouth stayed closed and my foot stayed put. "It's nice to meet you, Helen."

We sat down and she ordered a green tea. Her posture remained straight and tense, her purse still hung on her shoulders. It was as though she were springloaded to leave at the slightest whim. I was used to this, of course, taking no offense. Similar symptoms abounded in all manuscript consultations.

"I'm a little nervous," Helen said, watching with foreboding as I took out her marked-up manuscript from my attaché. "Actually I'm really nervous. I know I paid for this. I need this… it's just…"

"I understand. I do." The caffeine buzz widened my smile by several teeth and I hoped she found it more empathetic than patronizing. "Before I say anything, though, just indulge me and tell me some of your intentions and thoughts you had about the book. What you were going for."

Helen's green tea came and she picked it up and blew on it. I could tell she was quickly organizing her thoughts. Where to start? Indeed, I knew the feeling.

Since becoming part of the faculty at the university's English Extension Program, I'd been doing formal manuscript consultations for writers whose wallets could take the fee (a fee which wasn't unreasonable, but, against my protest, had been raised three times since the service began). In addition to the extra income, it was a great way to feel back in the game during my slumps, particularly when a slump lasted as long as this one. The full-throttle editing and the intimate one-on-one nature of consulting put it a notch above teaching, which never got my hands properly dirty—in a creative sense.

"I suppose I wanted to give myself one of the biggest challenges I could think of," Helen said. "I guess that's rather ambitiously silly, given it's my first novel. But I can't tell you how proud I am of myself for finally finishing it. I'm sure you know how it is."

"I certainly do. It's an orgasm for your brain. All the black gangly doubts and thoughts are washed away the moment you dot that last period. At least for a while." I thumbed through the manuscript. "I can see it was ambitious. And it's admirably original, I've got to say. To write from the perspective of the gerbil in the cage. His take on the whole… goofy family affair."

"Believe it or not, I think I did that for refuge, more than anything. Having experienced a lot of what happens between the couple in this story, I knew that if I tried writing it from either person's point of view that I'd probably be subject to the whim of my own biases. Putting the story through the eyes of something completely objective, not even human, helped ground myself. As weird as that sounds."

"No," I said, nodding. "I can see what you're saying."

The consultation lasted a little over the ninety-minute mark, and it was a very friendly and stimulating back and forth, a reminder of why I enjoyed this process so much when I found a good writer and a good person behind the words. Unfortunately in my experience, too many people have entrenched, uncompromising visions for their work, which I understand.

Towards the end of the meeting, I handed Helen her manuscript, as well as the five separate pages of notes I'd taken. She took it all gracefully, though I could tell she tried her best to conceal the winded look in her eyes.

"By the way," she said, as we got up to leave. "I was going to mention this earlier, but we got off to the races on my stuff. After I read your biography on the faculty page I bought a copy of *Emerald Moon*. I thought it was brilliant. I think that's also what made me so nervous. Sorry."

"Don't be silly," I said. "And thank you very much."

"Are you working on anything now?" Helen asked. "Or is that a question I shouldn't be asking? Some writers think it jinxes them to talk about works in progress."

"I'm not at all superstitious, so I'd gladly tell you if I had something cooking. But I'm afraid I'm in a dry spell."

"It'll come back," she said. "It'll ambush you, like it did for me." As we headed towards the exit I held the door open for her and she smiled at me, then added, "I swear, inspiration comes from the most unlikely places."

***

"She said it was the most violent she's seen him," Suzie said. As she spoke, she gently stabbed the chopsticks into the mound of food before her. Some part of her always needed movement to think. What part of her moved was context sensitive, and depended on the gravity of the subject. "When she asked him to stop tapping the pen he threw it at her, then picked up the chair and hurled it across the room. We're lucky it didn't hit anyone."

"The other kids aren't giving him a hard time, right?" I said, chewing. The greasy fast food noodles were becoming less appetizing to me, but I ate out of anxiety. It was something to do.

"No, not too much," she said. "They've got their own problems and, from what Ms. Sommers has told me, they're pretty tolerant of him. They stay out of each other's way. It also doesn't hurt she has fewer kids during summer sessions." Suzie swallowed. I could tell more words were tumbling down from behind her eyes. "But she says his behavior's been getting worse. She says he's more restless."

Suzie sighed, long, hard. "I guess we should be thankful Aaron lives in this day and age. Couple decades back and they probably would've thrown him into an institution. And kids were much less understanding about that kind of stuff."

"No one really knew about it," I said.

"We don't know much about it now," Suzie said. "But there's always a place to start."

We spent the rest of the meal in silence, the two of us picking our way through the dishes, slurping and munching down most of it under the dim glow of the kitchen light. Was this how Suzie and I were to spend the rest of our days? Had our bond been pruned to one lone connective fiber? Our marriage corralled into the tight, dark quarters of our son? She never mentioned much of anything else—not sincerely, anyway. All of it was obligatory, questions of my day or my work offered with whatever breath she had left. But I couldn't be too selfish. I was the one who got to escape more often. Suzie worked part time for a website and had flexible hours, and would sometimes stay home when Aaron became particularly adamant about not going to school.

After dinner I went to see Aaron in his room. The door was partially closed. I pushed it open and the hinges squealed. Aaron didn't move from his position on the floor by the bed, where he drew feverishly with markers and colored pencils on a large pad of bond paper. His auburn hair was stiff and greasy, his tongue pressed against the side of his mouth, and his entire body bobbed back and forth as if he needed to go to the bathroom but was waiting until he got something just so. The boy embodied diligent concentration.

I stood in the doorway for a moment, watching him as he alternated every few strokes between colors or media, his fingers dancing in the interim between selections. Suzie moved about downstairs.

Does he know I'm here? I thought. Does he know I'm here at all?

I moved in and sat on the bed. "Hey, bud."

His eyes shifted slightly, but his head remained at the same angle, gaze cast downward.

"Hi," he said.

"Mom was telling me you had an incident today," I said.

He kept bobbing, scribbling. Said nothing. The page was half full of spirals and lines of all colors. Aaron loved patterns and symbols. In fact, the most in his nine years that I'd ever been able to connect with him was when I gave him a box of Tangrams, a Chinese puzzle of arranging geometric shapes into position to create a specified image. He proved much better at it than I. Puzzles often opened a window into him, but neither Suzie nor I knew what he intended with this abstract art of his, if it was a game of his own make or just for disordered fun. I thought perhaps it was his preferred language, his own communiqué, codified.

"We've talked about listening to Ms. Sommers," I said firmly. "You know Mom and I don't like hearing about those kinds of things. And you could hurt someone doing that. You know better not to throw things."

Silence.

"Aaron."

More silence. He continued drawing. I had experienced this many times with him and knew not to take it too personally. He was fortified within himself, in many respects locked out of the world, and he couldn't help it. But, for whatever reason, I couldn't help the intense surge of frustration and resentment that flooded me. Before my rational mind had time to catch up, I'd taken Aaron's wrist and ripped the marker from his hand. I tried to force eye contact as he thrashed and screamed and clubbed my arm with his free hand.

"Aaron stop it," I said. "Listen to me. *Listen* to me."

He wailed and tears bubbled in his eyes. I heard Suzie start up the stairs.

"What's going on?" she cried.

I released him and he scurried away, then grabbed handful of markers and crayons—most of which were uncapped—and began throwing them at me. I moved back as they clattered against the mirrored closet doors behind me and tumbled across the carpet. One left a long red mark across the cuff of my trousers.

Suzie appeared in the doorway.

"Rich, what's wrong?"

"Go away!" Aaron screamed. "Go away!"

"I was… talking to him about what happened."

"Aaron," Suzie said, moving closer to him. "Aaron calm down. It's okay."

I stood there, pissed with myself, feeling like some slack-jawed newbie on the first day of a tough job. But then, every day was the first day of a tough job when it came to Aaron—a hazy, amorphous prospect from one hour to the next, even one moment to the next. It was frightening thinking the drawbridge might always be up, the fog between us immutable no matter how hopeful the occasional ray of sunlight might make us.

Suzie and I didn't speak much the rest of the night. I went downstairs to my study and she went to bed an hour after Aaron, without saying goodnight. I stayed in my study until two in the morning. I was always a nocturnal writer and in my heyday could make it till sunrise. Even if I could I wouldn't pull such a thing nowadays, though maybe that'd depend on the idea driving me.

But the moon and the dark did nothing for me that night, as they hadn't in years, and after two hours of trickling out a single paragraph, I deleted it. My tank was empty, and at some point I leaned back in the office chair and fell asleep. It was there I slept until the blinds were yellow with early sunlight.

***

Much of that summer in Los Angeles was gray, frosted with the marine layer that eddied in and loitered, sealing the city in a dim shade of Tupperware. Though commonly dubbed "June Gloom," the pattern usually extended far into July and even August. Strangely, the beginning of autumn often becomes warm by comparison, the sun hastily compensating for its spotty presence at a time it was most expected and appreciated.

That fall I was teaching two classes, one on playwriting and another on the history of the novel, the latter being one of my favorite subjects because its first big focus—once we'd covered the antecedents like Homer through Chaucer—was Cervantes, whose Don and Sancho remain, at least to me, largely unmatched in their philosophical and psychological exuberance.

"I perceive everything I say as absolutely true," says the Man of La Mancha, "and deficient in nothing whatever, and paint it all in my mind exactly as I want it to be." I envy the clarity of that cockeyed wisdom.

Don Quixote has always been one of the most healing of books for me. I suppose if I can't properly mount an explanation for precisely why this is so, I shouldn't teach the book, let alone call myself a writer. But there are truly some things that defy words. And why shouldn't that be? They are the things that keep writers writing, struggling to capture them in finely woven fishnets of language.

Given my happy absorption in the novels I planned to teach that fall, I felt less inclined to get my hands dirty with a consultation. Certainly I wouldn't turn away a project if the sample pages were promising, but I was more selective. In the first month I received from Kathy at the consultation office two ten-page samples, one a romance and another a science fiction. I turned them both down.

Then, a week or so shy of Halloween, Kathy called me about a new prospective manuscript.

"It's called *History's Amnesia*," she said. "*The Missing Pieces of the Past*."

"Doesn't sound like a novel," I said. A doe-eyed twenty-something, Kathy was one of the sweeter people I'd met on campus. She was bright and well-read, and a nice mixture of youthful innocence and realist. She also clearly had a thing for me, which is why I kept my distance. It was also why she came to me first for nearly every project that crossed her desk.

"It's written rather journalistically," she said. "Like a history book. But the synopsis sounds kinda fantastical. It mentions Atlantis."

I chuckled. "Okay. Interesting."

"Want me to send it over?" she said, with a slightly cartoonish inflection.

"I'd think if it's nonfiction—or trying to be—it'd be better for Ralph Broadwell or John Morgan. One of the guys in that circle."

"It doesn't specifically say one way or the other, though I'm sure it's leaning towards nonfiction."

"Hmm."

"So it doesn't look good to you?" She almost sounded hurt. I knew Kathy loved giving me things I enjoyed. She'd recommended more books to me than anyone else. Unsurprisingly, she was also one of the more vocal proponents of me writing another novel. Suzie used to be in that group, but hadn't been for years—the most I'd hear nowadays were offhand comments about writing short stories again for quick extra cash.

"No, I can check it out," I told Kathy.

"Great! I can bring over the book if you'd like. Just dip your toes in. If you want it, I'll tell the author."

"I know the score," I said amusedly. "What's the author's name?"

"Harold Byron, Ph.D."

The name rang a bell, but I had no idea why.

"Hey," said Kathy. "Would you like to join Mae and me for a drink? After I give you the book?"

"That sounds fun," I said. "But I think I'll take a rain check."

***

We homeschooled Aaron for most of his grade-school years. His teacher was Steve Rowen, a close friend of mind since college. Steve had been laid off from a middle school where he'd taught science. Aaron had known Steve his whole life and the acclimation went as smooth as we'd dared hoped. Steve had no experience working with special education students, but felt he could handle one, especially if it was a child he knew personally. He continued tutoring Aaron even when he was hired by another school, though eventually opted out to pursue a master's degree. Knowing Aaron strongly disliked change, we didn't hire anyone else, trying to do it ourselves as best we could, until we enrolled him in the emotionally disturbed class in a Santa Monica-based elementary school.

Aaron was in a class of eight other students who were intelligent like him, though less handicapped by aggressive behaviors. Two or three students sat at a table, except for Aaron—he had his own desk. Ms. Sommers ran the class with admirable compassion and enviable patience—which was why her recommendation for community day school, an even more specialized environment at the district headquarters, distressed me.

"They've got a new teacher," Ms. Sommers told us. "Her name is Maxine Waul. She's worked with autistic kids in her prior job as a counselor and is very nice, but firm. I'm sure she'll be better qualified and give Aaron a more suitable environment.

"I know it seems like I'm trying to pawn Aaron off," she continued. "But that isn't the case. I just want the best for him, as you do. I'm also worried about next year's class. This year's was pretty quiet and they were pretty good about leaving Aaron alone. But that's liable to change with the kinds of kids we get in here."

Suzie and I looked at one another, then at Aaron, who sat near the corner of the classroom on the edge of his seat, lost in drawing. As petty as it was, part of me didn't like the idea because it was yet another step removed from normal schooling. In the special ed class, he was at least at the local elementary school, surrounded by—if still buffered from — regular kids. If he went to this CDS place, he'd be among no one else but others like him, isolated, even further from the mainland.

"Mrs. Waul also encourages the arts," said Ms. Sommers, "and I know Aaron likes to draw. Every few months she has a little art show in her classroom. For the parents and kids."

Thankfully, Community Day School turned out a better prospect than initially feared. While normally resistant to change, Aaron appeared rather indifferent to the idea, though maybe his absorption in his drawing dulled the news. He responded in agreeable monosyllables.

"You'll be in a new classroom, with a new teacher and

new kids," said Suzie, with Ms. Sommers on the other side. I watched from behind. Suzie's face had held the same dull pallor for a while now.

Aaron didn't respond.

"Aaron," said Ms. Sommers.

"Yeah," he said, his gaze unbroken.

I wondered if he was listening. We often wondered that. And if he was, I wondered if his agreeability came more from concept than experience. Hearing about a new class was one thing—sitting in one was another.

All sorts of theories have of course been advanced about the source of autism, from genetics to childhood vaccines to the hyperconnected yet isolated age in which we live. All of these might be factors, then again maybe none of them are. There is also another theory I've come across and that's an evolutionary one, casting autistic kids as forerunners to a possible resultant branch of the direction humankind has undertaken in the last few centuries, and especially this past century. I can't say I remember much of the details, to be honest, but the notion's always both fascinated and scared me. Fascinated me to think Aaron might represent the seedling of a new age, scared me to think what kind of age it might be—scared me further to imagine we were essentially, for all intents and purposes, two different species.

***

On the eve of Aaron's first day in the new classroom, we were having grave doubts about the change. He was sullen, and would shout if given too much attention. He wanted solitude and we worried what the morning would bring. Earlier that day, we'd bought him some new art supplies to possibly help him warm up to the idea of this new teacher and classroom. Even though he used them and said "Thank you" (after we prodded him to do so) it helped little to bring us to him, or him to us.

We'd all met his new teacher, Maxine Waul, a mousy visage but a strong personality who seemed stable and intuitive, much like Mrs. Sommers. She was even able to fish a smirk from Aaron's face within ten minutes of meeting him. That alone, boosted by her colleague's testimony, raised our hopes and expectations, which saw no reason to dim the first week he was there. Surprisingly, the transition was much smoother than I imagined.

Meanwhile, I continued teaching and reading. Harold Byron's book, *History's Amnesia*, was a unique mixture of fiction and nonfiction. Historical accounts of civilizations, mostly Mediterranean and East Asian, were braided with new material describing tales of several lost civilizations in the Atlantic and Pacific. One from the Pacific shed light on coastal Native American colonies, such as the Chumash, and their mythic relations with those they called the First People. Beyond factual information available in other sources, the book filled its cracks with strange mythologies and folktales regarding places and creatures previously unheard of, then analyzed these stories against a historical backdrop. My admittedly stunted attempts to find these tales, or verify them elsewhere, proved futile. It was as if Byron had simply made them up.

It took me three weeks to finish the manuscript. Regretfully, since it wasn't a genre I was accustomed to, I didn't have many notes as I would on a regular novel. I wasn't sure why Byron didn't opt for a more suitable reader.

Efficient mediator she is, Kathy set up an appointment for us to meet once I told her I was ready. Apparently, Byron preferred a private place, so in lieu of the usual corner cafe we were to use my office.

The déjà vu was palpable when he walked in and greeted me. Byron was an older man, gray-bearded, and his unkempt clothes were an afterthought. The handshake was firm but brief, and eye contact was strangely limited. He spoke with cautious affability.

"Have we met?" I said. "You look familiar."

"No," he said quietly, "I don't believe we've officially met, but it's nice to meet you."

"Likewise. Have a seat." We sat down, Byron perched on the edge of his seat—the familiar spring-loaded look. He opened a notebook he held, the inside of which was a blizzard of scrawls. "I must admit I don't have quite as much to say about a book like yours. My forte is fiction."

"These are folktales," Byron said with a hint of defensiveness.

"Oh, I know." I cleared my throat. "But would you mind extrapolating first a little? Tell me about why you wrote the book. Where'd it come from? Who's it for?"

Byron fidgeted, briefly showcasing something like reluctance.

"I want you to know that these stories came to me from a very special place," he said.

"Where's that?" I said.

"They were dictated to me. I transcribed them. Or, transcribed what I could remember."

Uh oh. I worried Byron might start speaking of God or angels or channeled spirits, *a la* the Patience Worth case of the early twentieth century. Or, as I call all that unknowable stuff: the Big Whatever—in fact, that term has come to mean for me the entire Universe, seen or unseen.

"Who dictated it?" I asked neutrally.

Byron leaned forward. "The whales."

I blinked. "What?"

"You were there at the marina," he said. "I remember seeing you. The whale that was there for several days. It…spoke to me. Like the others. Told me more stories. Stories of a history of which we have little awareness, and almost no ability to comprehend."

That explains the rather alien nature of the stories, I thought. How most of them don't even feature humans, or familiarly human things.

"You're going to have to back up," I said. "Tell me what happened."

"You understand that whales are one of the most intelligent, yet enigmatic, creatures on Earth?" he said, unjustifiably on guard. Or maybe it was justified, given the outrageousness of his claims. "There are speech patterns among them as distinctive as Italian is from English, and the information quotient of some songs have been shown to rival that of *The Odyssey*. They've got lots to talk about. Lots to tell."

I nodded and kept my attention on the pages before me. I had to look as if I was humoring him, and I was, but I didn't particularly care if he knew that. I wanted to give him my feedback and leave it at that. But then again, wasn't this guy the personification of the quirky story, the odd anecdote, which I sought to fuel my ideas? Why was I in a hurry to get rid of him? Why did I find him more irritating than interesting? More obtrusive than conducive—conducive to what, one can't ever be sure with creativity. The ether—or perhaps the Big Whatever—has to fill in the gaps.

"Listen," said Byron. "It all sounds far-fetched I know, the idea of Atlantis, this 'lost civilization.' But a 'first people' myth permeates almost every society—even Native Americans have it. Plato was just one of many. There was something back there in the womb of history that inspired this knowledge. See, in thinking and writing and speaking of history, we crunch its millions and billions of years into seconds of speech, capsules of digestible time. Can we really imagine the expanse of a *million* years, even a hundred thousand, and still believe we have a firm grasp on whatever such years may have once contained and swept away? Modern humans are only thirty to forty thousand years old, right? Why isn't it possible another species could have evolved intelligence millions of years ago, in the droplet span of a few thousand years as we have, and been annihilated—either by natural or artificial means—so that scarcely any or no trace of them could now be found? And what if some glimmer of this civilization might have survived in the letters and tongues of future generations of our species, some itch in our consciousness, mere inklings easily enshrouded in myth and hyperbole?" Byron leaned back in his chair, projecting that kind of cock-eyed confidence I always imagined of *Don Quixote*. "We're all looking for it, some more than others. I know you are."

"Me. I'm looking for what? For Atlantis?"

"If you want to call it that."

"How do you know the whale, or whales, are… talking to you?" I asked.

"It started a while back," he said. "I got my degree in marine biology. I was particularly interested in whales and their form of communication, and began studying them. The more I did, the more I began to intuit patterns and thought processes, attributing verbs and nouns and even adjectives to their speech. That was the era I call grade school. Middle school came when I started having… I guess the best term is visions, or images, associated with the speech. They were hazy and chaotic. Symbols packaging meaning, like words. High school was when I learned to slit open the packages, make them somewhat coherent. That was when I actually started taken them down, writing this book. Unfortunately, by then my health was in a bad strait and I was retiring, no longer diving and all that."

"So the whale in the marina was more a matter of convenience?"

"I guess you could say that. The young ones love to tell stories. They've got tons, passed down from generation to generation. Like us. That book is only a fraction, I'm sure."

"Did you… jump in the water?"

He nodded. "I waited for nightfall. Then one of my old colleagues who owns a boat on the docks there let me in. All I was needed was a mask and snorkel."

Time was limited; knowing this discussion could easily spiral into a chasm of questioning, I rerouted it back to the actual book at hand. As the meeting wore on I gave him my feedback, then returned his marked-up manuscript.

"I'm not sure who will want this, to be honest," I said. "The stories are interesting, if less relatable because there's nothing really recognizable about them—"

"Why should there be? We're humans. They were another species. They were the ancestors of whales. Might as well be aliens."

"All right. But while it's very vibrant and very imaginative, they're not…" I bit my tongue, as I was about to say "not real," but could sense Byron knew I was headed that way. Then again, the fact they were recently fabricated was not too big a deal—like Tolkien, Byron had accomplished quite an imaginative feat. "The combination of fiction and non is very esoteric, and ungrounded."

Of course, I understood now why Byron didn't go to guys like Broadwell or Morgan for consulting—he didn't want the laughs.

"People need to hear these stories," he said. "They need to know the richness in their own backyard. They're deaf to it. And who knows how long it'll all be around, given where we're going."

Good luck, I thought. Despite Byron's age, youthful naiveté still thrived in him, which I kind of envied.

"Again, I think it's a very unique piece," I said. "I admire it. For a marine biologist you seem to have a good grasp on history and archeology, too. Not that I'm an expert."

"Thank you," he said. "I studied history in my undergraduate years. At least formally. Informally, I've been a historian my whole life."

"So the whales," I said, "never tell you where to look?"

"I don't even think they know," he said. "It was a different world then."

"I suppose so."

Our appointment went twenty minutes past the allotted ninety. It left me with an eerie taste in my mouth, as if I'd awakened from a weird dream, or had blacked out and could recall little of the last two hours.

Not long after Byron left, my phone rang. It was Kathy.

"How about that drink?" she said.

I hesitated, my smile incomplete but nonetheless a smile. "Doesn't sound like a half-bad idea."

***

Unlike prior invitations—all but one of which I'd turned down—this time I was not a third wheel to Kathy and one of her friends or co-workers. We were alone now, hunkering down in the lounge of a hotel within walking distance of the office. The ambiance was dim and elegant and I, of course, was acutely self-conscious. Yet I would've been just as self-conscious at one of the more crowded taverns dotting the fringes of campus.

What are you doing with her anyway?

We sat at a table by the window, melted into comfortable corduroy chairs affording front-seat views of the street. I ordered a glass of wine and Kathy got a martini.

We quickly entered the usual flow of literary and cultured conversation. Kathy always loved picking my brain about such things. Oddly, she never seemed to ask about more personal aspects, about Suzie or Aaron or anything. A couple bits had surfaced here and there, so I knew she was aware of that life, but it never particularly interested her. I wasn't sure if it was intentional or simply inconsiderate. Nevertheless, I wasn't resentful, at least not as much as I'd be if someone paid no interest (not even out of courtesy) to my writing. Not that there was much to discuss these days. Family was usually the topic of query anyway, and though it pains me to say this, it was nice to be with someone so removed—willingly or not—from all that, someone whose opening remarks might concern an idea for a novel rather than the name of a specialist.

Eventually, after rounding the ionosphere of abstraction and theory, Kathy and I turned earthbound and she asked me about my consultation with Byron.

"It was all right," I said. "Certainly one of the more memorable ones I've ever had. I didn't have too much to say on it."

"I was hoping maybe it would get your juices flowin'," Kathy said. "What I read of it was bursting with... I don't know, I guess imagination. But more. Color. Enthusiasm."

"No denying any of that," I said. "It's more what he told me that made the experience odd."

"What did he say?"

"He claimed they were dictated to him," I said, "by a whale."

"A whale? What? How?"

"Well, he actually said he'd been talking to whales for a while. But... he also mentioned the one in the marina. Remember? The stray one from a while back? That's what he said anyway. I don't know if he's just screwy or mounting some fairy-tale marketing campaign to show off the alleged Homers and Ovids of the sea. I guess he'd just be screwy in that case, too."

"All right." Kathy took a sip of her drink. "Sucks. I was wanting to go down and see that whale, but it left before I ever got around to it."

"It was a surreal sight," I said. "Seeing bars and condos and then—a whale. And actually I saw him down there."

"Who? Byron?"

I nodded.

"That's weird. Did you see him jump in and start chatting away?"

"Thankfully, no."

"That's still a weird coincidence," she said. "Maybe it's a sign."

"Stop it. You'll start to sound like him." I laughed and shook my head. "He says he gets signs and symbols. That's how he translates whale song."

Kathy made *a mas-o-menos* gesture. "I can believe that, to a certain degree."

"Excuse me?"

"Yeah. I'm not a woo-woo hippie or anything, but I'm good at reading symbolically. You know that. We've talked a lot about that stuff in literature. As Joseph Campbell said, not seeing beyond the symbols is like going to a restaurant and eating the menu."

I nodded and took a sip of my wine. "You're on your game."

"And it's not just in literature where I read them," Kathy said, blushing and dropping her eyes.

I hid my smile behind another sip of wine, but it was large enough so that it spread to my eyes and she saw it. She saw it and it went on from there.

Who knows what the hell I was doing, but I did it. After drinks, Kathy and I walked back to the campus parking lot, then caravanned to her place just three blocks away. We made love. All of it felt predetermined, as if I had some airtight contractual obligation with no escape clause. She was pretty much everything that had crossed my mind in slow-afternoon office fantasies—she percolated with an energy with which I'd long lost touch. All things I'd merely glimpsed behind her eyes, reserved in innocent touches, burst from every pore then, turned us inside-out and intoxicated the room with a tasteable, smellable, audible sex. I thought of nothing else as we rolled about, and the climax overcame me, cleansed me. Rejuvenated me.

I'm sure I was terribly rude in leaving—I think a goodbye slipped out, but given the fevered smear of my thoughts and movements, I'm still not sure. Tears came out of me on the way to the car, but I made effort to stop them. Suzie would be asking where I was. This time I had no story, an irony not lost on me. In a hopeful sign, however, she hadn't called my cell. Perhaps she figured I was working late.

My body felt under the sway of another force as I drove home, but it didn't feel external—it was familiar, as though a younger self were pulling an emotional Lazarus. I turned into the gas station where I bought a pack of Camels for my shuddering nerves. I hadn't smoked in ten years. Suzie would smell it on me, I knew. Another sign. Another story. I bought some gum to mask the ashen ghost of it on my breath, but it would cling everywhere, an odorous canary.

When I got home, Suzie and Aaron were seated at the kitchen table, hunched over homework, of which CDS—or maybe it was just Mrs. Waul—gave little. The sight of them opened floodgates of emotions in me, made it difficult to differentiate pity from guilt from love, but it was all there and it clutched at my chest.

"Hey guys!" I said. I went over and kissed the top of Aaron's head. He said nothing and continued bobbing in his chair. Then I kissed Suzie, steeling myself for the moment she mentioned the smokiness, readying the trite excuse that I'd merely been around smokers, but she just kissed me back and greeted me with a tired smile.

"I was about to call," she said. "Everything okay?"

"Yeah, everything's fine," I said. "I was reading papers and lost track of time." I went to get a glass of water. "Oh, and you wouldn't believe the consultation I had today." In those moments I was happy to have a topic of conversation from that day that defrayed—if slightly—the mental energy focused on what had happened with Kathy.

"Let's talk later," Suzie said. "I'm just helping Aaron patch up some things on this book report."

As a class they were reading Lois Lowry's *The Giver*. "I can help. Or pitch in."

Before Suzie could respond Aaron fervently shook his head, his gaze honed on the center of the table.

"No," he said. "No, no, no."

Suzie looked at me with empathy, but also—or so I perceived—with a little validation. A little hubris. Maybe I was reading too much into it, as I was wont to do with things, books or people. Maybe she knew. Maybe she had picked up on it that fast. Maybe it was bound to become the Great Known Unspoken, a successor to my mother's affair that had haunted my childhood home for years growing up.

Unsure whether it was the sexual cleanse from Kathy, or the nicotine, or both, that night I sat in my study and wrote ten stutter-footed pages. It was the most I'd done in a long time and I was happy to just get it out, regretful though I was knowing it came—probably—from such shitty behavior. But like my client Helen said, you never know where or when this stuff will ambush you.

***

I stopped doing consultations after the incident with Kathy. I wasn't entirely sure it would do any good, but figured it was a start, a punishing deprivation of two things for me—editing and seeing her—that would hopefully give us much less reason to interact. She was young and fickle, anyway.

Likely her job in the office was a layover, a way station, and she wouldn't be there much longer. When she left, perhaps I'd get my hands dirty again—the good way.

Byron's book was the last one I consulted on.

Many times over that year I thought I would break down in front of Suzie, unleash everything acidic in me—not just the indiscretion with Kathy but all of it, my borderline resentment of Aaron, of her, my life. But I kept it reined in, allowing it to bleed across the raw pages of my new short story, the complete direction of which I'd yet to grasp. Nevertheless, I knew I had to codify my confessions, attire them in metaphor and subtlety. Because I often read into others' work, I'd always been slightly paranoid about people doing the same thing with mine, especially those who knew me. Suzie wasn't particularly that type, but she was smart and she sometimes did ask questions—I had to submerge my issues deep enough to avoid overt detection.

I wasn't able to hide the smoking for long, however. Suzie was more understanding than I imagined, though she certainly wasn't happy, preferring not to indulge in much physical intimacy while I was on the habit's ashy hook. I explained it was a good synaptic enhancer, that it helped me think, put me in touch with my dusty old muse, and while she empathized and was glad to see me writing again, she still stood her ground. Mercifully, the habit didn't mutate into the addiction of years past—I found I could more or less turn it on and off.

Not long into the spring semester of the following year, Maxine Waul sent home announcements of a small classroom art show. She told us Aaron had picked out three pieces to display, the maximum for each student. We hadn't seen them, as he'd done them in class, but I could tell he was looking forward to it.

"Can't wait to see your stuff, bud," I told him, squeezing his shoulder.

Fingers dancing idly in the air, looking straight down, Aaron's face nonetheless lighted with a small smile. "Yeah," he said.

It started at five. Mrs. Waul greeted us and the several other parents who showed up. We milled around the room, taking in the little propped-up exhibits of everything from chalk pastel drawings to watercolors. Mrs. Waul encouraged "freedom of medium," as she proudly informed us.

Aaron's pieces were all done on regular-sized white typing paper, glued to cardboard frames. As usual they were mostly scribbles and shapes, two of them more rounded and organic in their content, the third more geometric. The coloring, while versatile, was erratic. On one of them I noticed a tessellation, one of those repeated, strung-together images that flow naturally into themselves. The hallmark of Escher.

Another mother moseyed on over next to me.

"Your son sure likes to tell a story," she said, smiling. "Has me crawling all over the place, twisting and turning and seeing new things."

"Thank you." I'm not denying it was a nice thing to hear, but I only knew that in the abstract. Personally, experientially, it was a dreary thing to hear. This person came off knowing more about Aaron than I did.

Passing by Mrs. Waul's desk, I noticed a paperback sitting atop several other books that, to my informed sensibilities, looked self-published. The title was lettered in a recognizable standard font, and the cover depicted a modern skyline stretched above the sea. Shimmering in the water was the inverse reflection of the cityscape, though it wasn't an accurate reflection but one of ornate, archaic architecture that looked like a cross between Aztec and Arabic.

It was *History's Amnesia: The Missing Pieces of the Past* by Harold Byron, Ph.D. I gathered he must have skipped traditional publishing and gone straight to a vanity press.

"Where'd you get this?" I asked Mrs. Waul, picking it up as she walked by.

"Oh, that was recommended to me by a former colleague," she said. "She told me one of her kids loved the stories. I haven't looked through it much myself yet. I was going to this weekend."

I was about to elaborate on Byron's consultation, but for whatever reason a big part of me didn't want to. I was saved the trouble of deciding when another parent snagged Mrs. Waul's attention.

I went over to Suzie, who sat beside Aaron. "I'm going to step out for a smoke."

"Okay," she said mechanically.

"Aaron, I'll be back, buddy."

No response.

The night was velvet and clear, a starry population I hadn't seen over Los Angeles in many years. I regretted adding a smoky, if tiny, pollutant to it.

Why did everything feel so out of control? It was as though I were a whipping boy for some onstage performer, slugged for what this person in my skin was doing or thinking. Smoke came out of me. Affairs came out of me. Stories came out of me and I couldn't grasp any of it. I felt knocked about, as if something had shanghaied the core stuff out of me and left the rest to drown. With every stroke, it slipped further downstream.

But I suppose at some level we all create these things ourselves. We are all artisans of the same medium, carving, crafting, chiseling from the same shapeless mold what we want. We have the same skills, just varying instruments through which they are implemented.

And who knows, such things might not be unique to the human race. We might be just one instrument with which the Big Whatever is trying to plumb its own recesses, pattern itself back to coherence, and at the same time it has employed upon the same task millions of other eyes and ears of all sets and sizes. And, in very rare leaps, maybe two entirely different ears can become synchronized, a step toward cohesion, to a time when we might be able to confidently remark that everything we perceive is true, deficient in nothing whatever, and painted exactly as desired.

ABOUT THE AUTHOR

Mike Robinson is the award-winning author of multiple books including the trilogy *Enigma of Twilight Falls*, *The Prince of Earth*, *Dreamshores: Monster Island* and more. He is also an active screenwriter, illustrator and producer, as well as a charter member of The Greater Los Angeles Writers Society and a freelance book editor. He's been a lover of all things odd and creepy since penning his seminal *Aliens Landed In My Backyard!* at age seven.

www.mike-robinsonauthor.com